ENCHANTED

THE ROGUES SERIES BOOK 4

TRACIE DELANEY

Edited by StudioEnp

Proofreading by Katie Schmahl, Jean Bachen, and Jacqueline Beard

Cover art by *Tiffany @TEBlack Designs*

ENCHANTED

BOOK FOUR IN THE ROGUES SERIES

Wanted: Companion for reclusive billionaire. Apply online now.

It should be so easy. A twelve month contract with a fat bonus at the end—providing I don't quit.

Except when something looks too good to be true, it usually is.

Little did I know how interwoven my life is with his.

Saving him might cure my own crushing guilt.

Or it could break us both.

The question is—am I brave enough to find out?

A NOTE TO THE READER

Dear Reader,

Wow, look at us! Here we are at book 4 in this series already. Can you believe it? The time is going so fast and as much as I love getting these books into your hands, especially given the amazing feedback I've had on this entire series, I can sense the end approaching—only two more to go—and I'm sad. These ROGUES are like family to me, and I adore spending time with them.

None more so than Upton and Belle. Their story is both heart-breaking and uplifting. It shows just how indomitable the human spirit is, and that, no matter how difficult life seems right now, there is always light and hope around the corner. One of the reasons I adore both writing and reading romance is knowing that however bumpy the journey, I'm going to get a happy ending.

I hope you enjoy reading Upton and Belle's story. I'd love to hear what you think about Enchanted once you're finished reading, either by leaving a review, or by joining my Facebook reader group Tracie's Racy Aces. Can't wait to chat to you over there.

In the meantime, dive in. Enjoy every moment. Upton and Belle are waiting.

Happy reading.

Love,
Tracie

BOOKS BY TRACIE DELANEY

The Winning Ace Series

Ace - A Winning Ace Novella

Winning Ace

Losing Game

Grand Slam

Winning Ace Boxset

Mismatch

Break Point - A Winning Ace Novella

The Brook Brothers Series

The Blame Game

Against All Odds

His To Protect

Web of Lies

The Brook Brothers Complete Boxset

Draven (A Brook Brothers Spin Off)

Irresistibly Mine Series

Tempting Christa

Avenging Christa

Full Velocity Series

Friction

Gridlock

Inside Track

Full Velocity Boxset (Books 1-3)

Control (A Driven World/Full Velocity Novel)

ROGUES Series

Entranced

Enraptured

Entrapped

Enchanted

Enthralled

Enticed

Stand-alone

My Gift To You

1

UPTON

"Upton, come on!"

Jenna almost wrenched my arm out of its socket as she hauled me through the crowd. "We have to get right to the front."

Her best friend, Verity, grabbed my other arm. "Better do as the birthday girl says, big brother."

I rolled my eyes but let them both pull me along. I pretended their teenage enthusiasm irritated me, but in reality, I'd do anything for my kid sister, and seeing her excitement brought me so much joy. I was brought up an only child. My mother died shortly after my eleventh birthday, and a year later, my dad remarried. Two years after that, Jenna arrived on the scene. She might only be my half sister, but I couldn't love her more.

My stepmother, Jenice, on the other hand… was a different prospect. We got along, but I'd always gotten the sense that she resented me, so I did my best to avoid her as much as possible.

Today was a milestone in Jenna's life, her sixteenth birthday, and she'd begged me for tickets to see Savage Groove, a rock band born and bred right here in Los Angeles, who were ending their hugely successful world tour in their hometown.

The concert hadn't even begun, and already the venue smelled of sweat and pot, but Jenna was at that age where those things didn't bother her in the slightest. Her life stretched out in front of her, full of endless possibilities. I'd decided to take a few weeks off from ROGUES—the global multi-billion-dollar business I co-founded and ran with my five best friends—this summer to spend as much time with her as I could. In August, she'd enter her junior year at high school —a crucial time in her education—and two brief years later, she'd head off to college, and I'd barely see her. Time had passed so fast. It seemed like only yesterday she was still in diapers.

The nearer we got to the front, the more the crowd closed in, pushing and jostling. About ten feet from the stage, the wall of people in front of us made it impossible to get any closer.

"This'll have to do, Jen," I said. "You've still got a terrific view."

If I'd had my way, I'd have gotten one of the executive boxes that ringed the stadium, but Jenna wanted to be right at the heart of the action, and I found it hard to refuse her anything. She'd always known how to wind me around her little finger.

"I suppose," she said. And then she clutched Verity, almost squeezing the life out of her. "This is so exciting. I can't wait for them to come on stage. Thanks so much for bringing me, bruv. You're the best."

I admit, I could be more than a little over-protective when it came to my sister. There were lots of teenagers here who'd come alone, but I preferred to keep her close, to protect her as much as I could, and concerts like this were too full of young men jazzed on drugs and hormones who'd love nothing more than to cop a feel and assume they'd get away with it in such a tight crowd.

Well, not on my fucking watch, they wouldn't.

"I have my moments," I said, grinning at her.

Her reply was lost in the screams that rent the air as the arena fell into darkness. Dry ice floated up toward the ceiling, and multicolored strobe lights flashed, hung from huge gantries above the stage. A heavy bass beat thudded, and the floor beneath our feet vibrated and shook.

The band appeared, and the cries from the audience increased in volume. The two girls jumped up and down, but their squeals of excitement were lost in the surrounding noise. A broad smile edged across my face as I watched her rapt expression as her eyes locked on the lead singer. He grabbed the mike and opened up with the song that'd catapulted them onto the global stage. They weren't my thing, but their popularity wasn't in question.

Thirty minutes into the concert, a stagehand brought a stool for the lead singer to sit on. The crowd fell silent. He began to sing a ballad, only him, a guitar, and a piano, a haunting tune about a life lost that gave me pause. I wouldn't have thought he had it in him to sing something so beautiful. Jenna and Verity had their arms around each other, swaying to the music, their heads almost touching. I stood behind, watching the band and them, a soft smile on my face.

A flash went off to my left.

Bang!

A fireball exploded, and a wave of heat knocked me to the floor.

Screams rang out. Fearful. Confused. Desperate.

The crowd surged. Mayhem and chaos everywhere.

A foot landed on my chest, and I groaned and instinctively curled into a ball.

Blood.

Red.

Everything's red.

What's happening?

I tried to sit up. Another heavy boot crushed me back down again.

Jenna!

I clambered to my feet, swaying. My shirt hung in tatters. Pain. Agonizing, tearing, hideous pain. All over. I couldn't pinpoint it to one particular part of my body. *It's bad.* I grabbed on to something. An arm. Leather jacket. I squinted.

"Get off me, man!"

The owner of the jacket shoved at me and then ran. I almost fell over but managed somehow to keep myself upright.

"Jenna," I yelled, panic sliding into my veins. Smoke filled my eyes and my lungs, and still the screams went on and on.

"Jenna!"

I couldn't see her or Verity anywhere. I glanced down. All around me, bodies lay strewn, some missing limbs.

So much blood. Nausea crawled into my throat.

What the fuck's happened?

And then I saw it. A strip of pink. *Jenna's shirt is pink.* I stumbled over, falling to my knees. "Jenna." I pushed hair, matted with blood, off her face. She groaned. "Don't move," I ordered. "Help's coming."

"Upton."

Her breathing rasped, her lungs rattling.

"Don't try to talk. Just stay very still for me, okay?"

Her eyes flickered. "Verity."

I shook my head. "I can't see her."

"Hurts."

I felt around for her hand, found it, and rammed my eyes shut. "I know, honey. I know. Please, just keep real still for me, okay? Help is coming."

"I'm scared, Upton. Don't let me die, please."

"You're not going to die." I brushed another bloody clump of hair off her forehead, but more blood came, splattering her forehead, and then I realized it was coming from me. I pressed a hand to my face, touching a gaping wound in my cheek.

Fuck.

The arena was emptier now, save for the injured and dead lying all around. High-pitched ringing pierced my eardrums. It had to be a bomb. There was no other explanation. *God help us. Help my sister.* I turned my attention back to Jenna again. When she breathed in, a horrible gurgling sounded in her chest.

"Stay with me, sis. I'm here. Stay with me."

Sirens blared in the distance, slowly creeping closer. I might've blacked out, not sure, but the next thing I remembered was a couple of paramedics loading me onto a stretcher.

"Jenna, my sister. Is she... is she...?"

The female paramedic squeezed my hand. "Let's just get you to the hospital, okay?"

I coughed, and pain ripped up my back. I cried out, damn near blinded from the agony.

"Here, this should help with the pain."

A sharp prick jabbed the back of my hand, and my eyes drooped.

~

A throbbing in my cheek forced me awake. I raised a hand to my face and came into contact with what felt like thick padding. I pressed and hissed through my teeth. Fuck, that hurt.

Dad's face swam into view, worry mingled with relief swirling in his eyes. "Oh, thank God. You're awake. How are you feeling, son?"

Confusion made it difficult to think straight. My brain felt as if it'd been stuffed with cotton wool, a fog that meant nothing made any sense.

"What happened?" I muttered. Christ, who's voice was that? Hoarse, cracked, a horrible rasping sound.

And then, in a flash of horror, the memories came roaring back.

"Jenna," I whispered, trying to sit up. "Where's Jenna?"

Dad urged me to lie back down. Silent tears tracked their way down his face. Rivers of them.

I'd only seen my father cry once. At my mother's funeral.

A vise closed around my chest, and my lungs flattened.

"Just tell me. Where is she?"

Dad shook his head and then shifted his gaze onto the blank wall directly ahead of him.

A pain like no other welled up inside me, filling every space with this awful hollowness, an empty pit of despair. No. Not Jenna. Not my sister. She couldn't be dead. Her light shone too brightly for it to have been snuffed out as easily as smothering a candle. I never got to tell her one last time how much I loved her, how happy she made me. I'd never get to hug her again, or hear her girlish giggle, or watch her eyes shine with pleasure at the simplest of things.

"It should've been me." A sob crawled into my throat, but I pushed it down. "Not her. Not Jenna."

Dad wrapped his fingers around my hand. I could feel the warmth on the outside, but inside, I was nothing but ice.

"Don't say that, Upton. Please don't. You're my son. My only son, and I love you so very much."

A tear dampened my cheek. I left it there. "Where's Jenice?"

Silence greeted me. I looked at Dad, and his eyes were bleak and filled with a pain I couldn't bear.

"She blames me, doesn't she?" When he didn't reply, I nodded. "That's okay. I blame myself."

"No," Dad exclaimed. "It wasn't your fault. Jenice... she's hurting. We're all hurting. Just give her some time."

Time wouldn't solve this, and worse, I didn't blame Jenice for hating me. I hated myself. I'd taken Jenna to that concert. I bought her the tickets for her birthday. I'd made that decision. If I hadn't, then she'd still be here with us.

I'd lost Jenna, and I'd effectively lost my Dad, too, no matter what he said. Jenice would need him, and he'd go to her, be what she needed. And I already knew that what she'd need was never to see my face again.

"What about Verity?"

For the second time, Dad's eyes lowered, and then he quickly shook his head.

"It was a bomb, wasn't it?"

"Yes."

I looked away. "How many dead?"

"Ninety-four."

"Jesus Christ."

Another tear dripped down my face, then a third and a fourth. A flow I couldn't stop. Why had I survived? What was so fucking special about me that I was spared and yet so many others lost their lives? The ache inside my chest increased to agonizing, hideous pain. *I can't bear it. I can't do this. Please, fuck, please, just let me go.*

"How long? How long have I been here?"

"Two days. They operated on you for seven hours, Upton. You had so many pieces of shrapnel buried in your skin, and one narrowly missed your spinal cord. You're lucky to be alive, but you are alive. And that's all that matters."

"Is it?"

I gingerly touched the padding on the side of my face. I was probably scarred for life, but who cared? Jenna was gone. She'd never graduate college or meet a man she loved enough to marry, or have kids, and a fulfilling career. My sister was dead, and every time I looked in the mirror, the wounds I bore would remind me of the dreadful truth.

"The boys are here," Dad said. "All of them. Garen flew back from Dublin, and Sebastian came all the way from London. They're desperate to see you."

I shook my head. "Tired." The thought of seeing my friends, watching their faces crumple in sympathy for their poor buddy with his fucked-up face, scarred body, and ruined life. I'd choke on the pity if I saw them now. "Maybe tomorrow."

Or maybe never.

2

One year later

Belle

Come on, lights. Change, damn you.

Cars zipped along the street, the crosswalk sign obstinately stuck on red. I glared at it as if shooting daggers in its direction would have any sway and checked my watch for the umpteenth time, cursing the stupid bus for being late. I should have taken an earlier one and saved myself a lot of stress as well. If I landed this job, two things were going to happen: one, I'd buy Zak an electric wheelchair, and two, I'd get a blasted car.

A drop of water landed on top of my head, followed by a second and a third. I glanced at the gray clouds rolling in. *Are you kidding me?*

Risking my life—and a fine I couldn't afford for jaywalking—I darted into the traffic, ignoring the blaring horns and rude hand gestures, and made it to the other side unscathed. As I ducked inside the hotel, the heavens opened. Phew. Lady Luck was with me for once. Arriving for an interview looking like I'd showered in my clothes wasn't a good idea.

I riffled through my purse and pulled out the details the agency had sent me. *The Mercury Suite, eleven a.m.* I checked around, searching for directions. Ah, there. I crossed the vast lobby and peered up at the chrome-and-black signage. After following the arrows, I eventually found the right room. I was still five minutes early, but never mind. Better early than late. I rapped twice on the door.

"Come in."

I pressed down on the handle and entered. My gaze fell on two men dressed smartly in dark designer suits and power-color ties. I managed to suppress my astonishment. They were far younger than I'd imagined. When I'd applied for the job, I'd carried out scant research, discovering the owners of this hotel chain also owned several other successful businesses. Somehow, I'd envisaged them to be in their forties or fifties, but these guys couldn't be more than thirty. I wished I'd reviewed their website more thoroughly now. I hoped they hadn't noticed my surprise.

"Hi, I'm Izabelle Laker. I'm here for the interview."

Both men rose to their feet and fastened their suit jackets, then extended their hands.

"Thanks for coming, Miss Laker. I'm Sebastian Devereaux, and this is my business associate, Garen Gauthier. Please take a seat."

I shook first Sebastian's hand and then Garen's and pulled out a chair. Smoothing my skirt beneath my thighs, I sat.

"Would you like some water?"

"Please," I said, only then realizing how dry my throat felt. After a few tiny sips and a couple of deep breaths, my shoulders relaxed. I could totally do this. I didn't usually get nervous before interviews. It had to be the salary on offer, almost twice what I earned in my current role as an assistant manager of a retirement home. I loved my job, and I'd be sorry to say goodbye to my residents, a lot of whom were like family to me, but I had to put Zak's wellbeing first, and the money being offered would make such a difference to our lives. Besides, from what little I knew, this sounded like an easy gig.

Sebastian kicked off the interview, scanning down a sheet of paper I recognized as my resume. "I see you've made a career out of caring for people, Miss Laker." He lifted his chin and smiled. "What is it that appeals to you so much?"

I smiled in a way that I hoped came across as being professional and friendly. "I've always found a lot of personal joy and satisfaction in caring for others. I've known since I was small that I wanted to work in this sector in some capacity."

He nodded and jotted something down on a white, thinly lined pad.

Garen, the other interviewer, asked me a question next. Back and forth they went, their questions drilling deeper and deeper. These guys were clearly outstanding interviewers. Then again, they must have done it a lot.

I held my own, although their faces gave nothing away. Finally, after almost an hour, Sebastian put down his pen and rested the edges of his knitted hands on the table.

Phew. Almost there. Don't screw up now.

"Do you have any questions for us?"

"Um, yes, just a couple. The agency told me the role is to act as a companion. Could you tell me more about the man I'd be caring for? Is he your grandfather?" I glanced between the two of them.

Sebastian's smile held a hint of sadness. "Not exactly. He's only thirty-one."

"Oh." I sat a bit straighter and nibbled on my lip. Gah! You'd have thought the agency would have told me. I just assumed, given the role of *companion*, it was for an elderly man who'd lost his wife, perhaps.

"Sorry, the agency never said." *And I didn't ask.*

I should have asked.

"Don't worry," he said. "We purposely kept the details scant on the brief." He glanced at Garen who gave the smallest nod. "Upton is our best friend, and our business partner. Together with three of our other best friends, we run a global corporation, ROGUES. You're sitting in one of our hotels, but that's only part of our brand. Upton runs our West Coast operations, or rather he did up until a year ago."

My interest piqued, and I automatically leaned forward. "What happened a year ago?"

Another glance at his business partner. Another confirmatory nod.

"Upton, along with his sister and her best friend, attended the Savage Groove concert."

My heart all but struck the floor, and a jagged wound reopened in my chest, one I tried to stitch together on a daily basis in the knowledge it never took much to rip it open again.

I hadn't expected a bloodbath today, though.

"Oh God," I whispered.

Sebastian continued, almost as if I hadn't interjected. "His sister and her friend both died. Upton survived. And he's never forgiven himself for it. Since then he's dropped out of life, becoming almost a recluse. He's not interested in anything. He's basically given up."

"The main thrust of this role," Garen explained, "is for the successful candidate to try to succeed where we've failed. To show him that life is worth living, to give him hope for the future. To be there if he decides to talk. He won't listen to us. We're too close to him, too much a reminder of what his life used to be like. There may be some light duties, but he has a full-time housekeeper who does most of the work, as well as a gardener slash handyman to take care of the externals."

Sebastian sipped his water, then refilled his glass from a jug in the center of the table. He held it up to me. I nodded, accepting a refill, too.

"Full disclosure, Miss Laker. We've hired several other people over the last nine months. Seven, to be exact. Some haven't done too badly. One lasted four weeks. Another didn't even make it through a single day. This isn't an easy job. Upton can be very difficult, and that's putting it mildly. At times, he's cantankerous and prone to terrible mood swings. At others, he's silent and withdrawn. The successful candidate will earn every penny of their salary putting up with him."

"Survivor guilt," I muttered, my voice almost inaudible judging by the frown that arrowed Sebastian's eyebrows inward.

"What did you say?" he asked, not unkindly.

I locked my gaze on his. "He's suffering from survivor guilt. That's a pretty tough place to be. His bad moods don't surprise me at all."

The two men shared another one of their secretive looks. I'd started to wonder if they were telepathic or, more likely, they just knew each other well enough to communicate without words.

"You sound as though you're speaking from experience," Garen said.

I glazed over, my mind pulling me to places I didn't want to visit. Dark places. I shook my head as if that simple movement had the power to push the thoughts away. It didn't. Keeping busy and helping others was the only medicine I'd found that came close to giving me a shred of peace.

I'd wanted this job badly, mainly for the money. Earning a bigger salary meant I could make life better for Zak. Now that I knew more about Upton Barrick, I wanted it even more.

No, not wanted.

Needed.

Had to have.

Dammit, would have.

"We all have our demons, Mr. Gauthier. I'm aware that hiring anyone is a risk to an employer, and you haven't had the best of luck so far, but if you give me a chance, I know I can help your friend. I have an abundance of patience, I'm not easily scared away, and he can yell at me all he likes. It still won't be as bad as some of my elderly patients suffering with dementia. Now *they* know how to cuss someone out. You have to be tough to survive in my line of work."

His eyes bored into mine, and it took a huge effort not to turn away, despite what I'd just said about being tough. Intimidating didn't even begin to cover it when describing his expression. I'd bet he was fearsome in his business dealings.

I shifted in my seat, held back a shiver of disquiet, and kept my eyes on him, refusing to even blink, my face open but not defiant.

"He will do everything in his power to make you quit. You can bank on that."

I smiled. "I like a challenge, Mr. Gauthier."

His lips curved at the edges, a barely there smile, but noticeable all the same. He shot a quick sidelong look in Sebastian's direction and whatever he saw sent him to his feet. He reached across the table and thrust out his hand. "Just as well, Miss Laker, because you have a helluva task ahead of you."

My lips parted, half in shock, half in utter delight. We shook hands. "You're offering me the position?"

"It appears so," he said.

I tamped down on the urge to punch the air—yeah, so not a professional response—and shook Sebastian's outstretched hand also. "Thank you so much. I won't let you down."

"A little bit of free business advice," Sebastian said. "Don't promise what you can't say with certainty you'll deliver, Miss

Laker." He added a grin and returned to his seat. "We'll have the contract drawn up today and couriered over. For every month you stay, we'll add a small bonus on top of your salary. If you somehow give us back our friend..." He trailed off, his gaze wandering to the window, almost lost in his thoughts. "If you perform a miracle, Miss Laker, I, personally, will ensure you are rewarded handsomely. But let me be clear; he will offer you more money than we are paying to leave. He's done it before, and he's nothing if not consistent." He laughed, but it came out as bitterness steeped in loss. "However, I warn you, if you accept his offer, you will be in breach of contract, and we will come after you with the full force of the law."

His geniality disappeared, replaced with a hard edge that hadn't been present until now. During the entire interview, he'd come across as far more amiable and friendlier than Garen, but it turned out both men were hard as nails. Unsurprising, really. No one reached the pinnacle of the business world without having a spine of steel and Teflon-coated broad shoulders.

"I'd never do that," I said, inserting a steeliness of my own to my tone. "I have both integrity and staying power in spades."

As well as my own reasons for wanting this role, which I don't intend to share with you or anyone.

His smile returned. "Good." He walked around the table separating us, then opened the door. "We'll be in touch."

I stood and shook his hand once more. "I look forward to it."

3

BELLE

Miracle of all miracles, the bus arrived right on time, which then meant I arrived at Upton Barrick's mansion in Malibu ready for my first day forty-five minutes early. The house was hidden behind an enormous set of oak gates, and the entire property was ringed by an eight-foot brick wall.

My gaze alighted on a keypad to the side of the gates, and I thought about letting myself in using the security code provided in the letter that accompanied the contract. However, the letter also stated that Sebastian Devereaux would meet me out front at eleven a.m. If they'd wanted me to use the code, they would have said. Pissing off my new employers on day one wasn't the best idea.

As the heat rose, sweat beaded along the back of my neck and between my boobs. I rummaged in my purse and managed to find a tissue. I turned my back in case any passing motorists saw what I was doing.

"Miss Laker."

I spun around. Unfortunately for me, I still had my hand inside my cleavage. I whipped it out, but not fast enough. Sebastian Devereaux greeted me with an arched eyebrow and a faint smirk.

"Oh, I wasn't expecting you yet," I said, stuffing the damp tissue into my jacket pocket.

"Clearly," he drawled, but his eyes twinkled.

Thank God. The man had a sense of humor.

"I caught an early bus. I didn't want to be late."

"Let's get inside, shall we? It's oppressively hot today." He tapped on the keypad, and the gates swung inward. He gestured to his car idling by the curb. When I stayed where I was, he smiled. "It's a long walk up to the house."

Oh.

I climbed in, and the air-conditioning blasting from the vents immediately cooled me. Sebastian steered the car up a winding driveway with a fairly steep incline that I wouldn't relish walking in the depths of winter, let alone on a hot summer's day. I'd need to get used to it, though. The bus didn't offer a door-to-door service.

"How are you feeling about today?" he asked.

Like throwing up or wishing I could skip past the next few days and get over day one struggles.

"Nervous," I admitted. "But excited, too."

He nodded. "He knows we're coming. Suffice to say he isn't happy."

"Then why does he let you in?" I asked, genuinely curious. "Couldn't he just change the code or refuse to answer the door?"

"He did, at first. Didn't do him any good, though. Now he's resigned to the fact we're not going anywhere, and no matter how much he tries to push us away, he's wasting his time." His face darkened, sadness tugging the corners of his mouth downward. "He's my best friend. I miss him terribly. We all miss him."

"He's still in there, somewhere, lost in his grief. He'll come back when he's ready."

The car stopped, and Sebastian cut the engine, shifting in his seat to face me. "Will he?"

It was hard to miss the spark of optimism in his eyes, but I'd guess he'd gone there a few times over the last year only to have his hopes dashed. I was so lucky to have Zak. Despite all he'd suffered, the one thing he'd clung on to was his steadfast belief that alive and unable to walk was a far better outcome than death. If he'd sunk into a deep depression like where Upton Barrick appeared to be, I wouldn't be able to take it. Guilt drowned me on the best of days. Zak's continued optimism allowed me to breathe, to cope with the terrible remorse that still gave me nightmares, even after all this time.

"I'll do everything I can." At least I understood his pain.

Sebastian's eyes dulled. "Okay, let's do this."

I climbed out of the car, and only then did I notice the house.

Wow.

I'd expected wealthy, especially with a Malibu address and the number of businesses this guy's company owned, but this...

A massive brick-built structure towered above me, three stories high. To the front, pristine gardens and colorful borders filled with summer flowers softened the appearance, and large trees offered dappled shade from the heat of the sun.

"Whoa. That's some house."

"It might as well be a prison," Sebastian said, his voice filled with so much sadness, my chest tightened. He inhaled deeply. "Follow me."

We entered the house through a large entranceway that had several doors leading off and a curved staircase which went up to the upper levels. I hurried after Sebastian, my heels clicking on the marble tiled floor, and arrived in an enormous kitchen, all sleek lines and contemporary design.

Sebastian introduced me to the housekeeper, Barbara, then motioned for me to follow him outside. "Come on. Let's introduce you to Upton." He flashed a smile. "Buckle up."

A prickle of unease took root at the base of my spine, and I furtively wiped my palms on my jacket. I'd dealt with difficult people before. I had the techniques, the coping mechanisms. All would be fine.

I hoped.

I caught sight of a dark-haired man sitting at a table, a parasol providing a little shade. He had his back to me, his gaze fixed on a point in the distance across an expansive backyard, as pristine as the front with grass so short and even, it could have been cut with scissors rather than a lawn mower. Sunlight glinted off an Olympic-sized swimming pool, and several loungers were dotted around.

"Upton," Sebastian called out, ambling over.

Upton didn't move. He didn't acknowledge us at all, his eyes still trained on a row of towering trees.

"This is Izabelle Laker," Sebastian continued, seemingly unperturbed by his friend's silent response.

"Hi." I moved into his line of sight. "Call me Belle."

He slowly turned in my direction, and his eyes latched on to mine. Whatever he saw on my face curled his lip into a sneer, and he snorted.

"Another rubbernecker," Upton snapped. "Go on, beautiful, take a good long look. Then fuck off."

"Upton," Sebastian lectured. "For Christ's sake, don't be such a dick."

The hairs on the back of my neck stood on end, and my hands coiled into fists. I had to force them to unfurl. They'd warned me the man was rude and crabby, but knowing and experiencing were two different things entirely. I breathed deeply through my nose and held the air in my lungs until the urge to hit back with a rant of my own subsided. I refused to allow him to get between me and Zak's wheelchair. It meant far too much to me.

Upton swiveled his chair around, giving us his back once more. As I calmed down, I silently cursed myself for not hiding my surprise, and then I cursed Sebastian for not warning me that Upton had a deep scar that ran from the edge of his eyebrow all the way down to his jawline. He must have gotten hit with shrapnel from the bomb. It didn't matter a bit to me, nor did it detract from his scorching good looks. Clearly, though, it mattered hugely to Upton Barrick.

Goddammit, he'd think I judged him. If only he knew I was in no position to judge anyone. I might not wear my scars on the outside, but that didn't mean they weren't just as deep, just as raw.

Great start, Belle.

I pulled out a chair directly opposite Upton, anticipating the possibility he might move his again in a show of defiance. When he didn't, I sat. "I'm sorry," I said.

He kept his gaze averted. "What for? I'm used to people ogling me like I'm a freak."

"You are not a freak."

He laughed, a short sharp bitter sound that held no mirth. "How do you know?"

I glanced up at Sebastian. "We'll be fine. I'll call if I need anything."

Upton's head snapped to me then. "You're not staying."

"I think you'll find that I am. Unless he tells me to go, that is."

Upton glared at Sebastian. "You take her with you right now or I'll—"

"You'll what?" I interjected ahead of Sebastian, grateful my voice didn't crack. I couldn't afford to show weakness in front of

Upton. I *had* to assert my authority to stand a chance of keeping this job for more than ten minutes. If I allowed him to walk all over me, I might as well quit right this second. "What is it that you'll do, Mr. Barrick?"

He locked eyes with me, although it felt more like we were locking horns. I held his gaze. If he expected me to back down, he was in for a very long wait.

"Trust me, you don't want to find out."

Shoving back his chair, he sprang to his feet. A magazine I hadn't noticed fell to the ground. He left it where it lay and stomped into the house, leaving me and Sebastian alone.

"That went well," I said, offering him a reassuring smile. "Go. It's for the best."

He nodded. "I'll be around for a week or so, but then I have to get back to London." When I arched an eyebrow in query, he added, "That's where I live. But Garen's only up in Vancouver. He can fly down here in a matter of hours, and I'm just a phone call away."

"Don't worry. I'll stay in touch." I felt the need to pat his arm reassuringly.

My eyes followed him back into the house, and then I leaned down and picked up Upton's magazine. *Investor's Weekly.* I smiled. He hadn't completely given up.

Now all I had to do was figure out a way to reach him.

4

Upton

Fuck's sake.

Another fucking do-gooder who thought they could fix me. Companion my ass. When would Sebastian get the fucking message and just let me be?

Over the last few months, it had become more and more evident that he thought shoving one gorgeous woman after another in my face would somehow fix me, when all it did was remind me of what I'd lost.

Women who looked like Izabelle Laker weren't interested in men like me who had a fucked-up face and a shattered body.

A broken heart.

It didn't matter anyway. I wasn't interested in her. Not in the slightest. The way my dick jerked when I set eyes on her was a physical reaction. And I could take care of that easily enough—alone.

I stomped through the house, whirling straight past Barbara who muttered something about dinner, and headed straight for my study. I flopped into the chair and closed my eyes, pinching the bridge of my nose.

When I opened them, my gaze alighted on a picture of me and Jenna, taken on her fifteenth birthday, just over two years ago, and a year before she died. I reached over to the bookcase and picked it up, staring into her amber eyes, almost a replica of mine except hers had this outer ring of brighter gold that always reminded me of the solar flares seen on countless programs on *National Geographic.*

The last year had passed by in a blur of self-recrimination, self-flagellation, crippling guilt, and a fervent yearning for the pain to stop. In those early weeks and months, it had crossed my mind to put an end to it on a daily basis.

What stopped me was Jenna. She'd had her life cruelly snatched from her by decisions I'd made, and the evil act of a terrorist hell-bent on destroying the freedoms of others. I owed it to my little sister to live with the pain. I didn't get to escape, to take the easy way out. Each day I suffered, and I welcomed it.

I brought the picture to my chest and hugged it. "Miss you," I whispered.

A shuffling noise alerted me to movement outside my study, and three seconds later, *she* appeared clutching the magazine I'd left out by the pool. I should cancel the subscription; I barely skimmed the thing when it arrived like clockwork each month, but cancelling took effort, and I didn't care enough to bother.

"You left this," she said by way of explanation.

I stared at her coldly, stood to return the picture to its rightful place, then sat back down. I angled my chair away from her, my message clear. Go. The fuck. Away.

"Is that your sister?" she asked.

My jaw razored from side to side. Same drill, different girl. Sebastian always told them my backstory. I guess he'd have to, although it still pissed me off. At first, they'd feel sorry for me, drown me in their pity, consumed with the certainty that they'd be the ones to fix me and secure the huge bonus I knew Sebastian offered for the first woman who jump-started my heart and brought me back to life. I briefly mused how long it would be until Izabelle Laker joined the other seven do-gooders Sebastian had organized and quit her post. My record was one day. I was still proud of that. The one who'd lasted the longest, Sitara, made it to thirty-two days. But eventually, even she couldn't take my dour moods and refusal to engage.

Silence was a powerful weapon. The business world had taught me that. And when silence didn't work, a burst of anger usually did the trick.

I'd assumed Sebastian would give up on me long before now, but the stubborn bastard clearly had other ideas. He couldn't keep this up forever, though. Sooner or later, he'd have to admit defeat. I prayed for that day, for the time to come when I'd be allowed to retreat into myself and disappear from the world. I was a virtual recluse already, only venturing out when absolutely necessary—usually to see a medical professional. On my last visit to the hospital, my doctor had told me I was probably looking at another few months of treatment, and then that was it. He couldn't do any more for me.

"She's the image of you," Izabelle said.

Her soft voice pulled me back to the present. I'd forgotten she was even here, and while I'd been lost in my head, she'd ventured into my office and gone over to the bookcase to peer at the picture of me and my sister.

I pushed my chair away from my desk, got to my feet, and very purposefully turned the picture around, away from her prying eyes.

"This room is out of bounds, as is my bedroom suite. As for the rest..." I shrugged. "Go where you like. Just keep away from me."

I walked off.

She followed.

"I'm here to stay, Mr. Barrick."

"That's what your predecessors said," I replied, heading for the stairs. I took them three at a time and marched down the hallway to my bedroom. For a little thing she moved fast, soon catching up to me. I opened my bedroom door, then spun around to face her. "Here's the line. Don't cross it."

I slammed the door in her face.

Two hours later, hunger drove me back downstairs. Even recluses had to eat, and I'd skipped breakfast. Quiet greeted me as I walked into the kitchen, and I breathed a sigh of relief. I didn't mind Barbara so much. She knew me well enough to read my moods and recognize when I was up for a little conversation versus craving solitude. This new woman, however, something about her set my teeth on edge. I had pretty good instincts, and right now they were firing up, informing me that this one wouldn't be as easy to break as the others.

Then again, everyone had a limit, and in the end, I'd discover hers—and then use it to my advantage.

I opened the fridge and grabbed a bowl of Cajun rice left over from last night's dinner. A rare smile touched my lips. Barbara was a woman who didn't like to waste food and often came up with creative ideas to make the most of every morsel. I added a few slices of chargrilled chicken to it and, grabbing a fork, I wandered into the backyard.

The second I stepped foot on the patio, I cursed. Izabelle was sitting there, nibbling on the smallest sandwich I'd ever laid eyes on. She heard me approach and set it down, then wiped her fingers on a napkin.

"Hi."

I could have spun on my heel and gone back inside. Two things stopped me: one, this was my fucking house and I could go where I pleased, and two, if I was to force Izabelle Laker to quit, now was as good a time as any to start.

"I hope you brought your own food," I said, the legs of the chair scraping as I pulled it out from beneath the table. "Provision of meals isn't part of the contract, and stealing is a criminal offense."

"How do you know what's in my contract?" she challenged. "You didn't draw it up."

Fucking woman.

Fucking Sebastian.

"As it happens, I did bring this myself. And if you ask me, downright rudeness should be a criminal offense, too, although lucky for you, it isn't, otherwise you'd be looking at a long stretch inside."

"I'm sorry," I said sarcastically.

"You should be."

She picked her sandwich up again and bit into it. A crumb nestled at the corner of her mouth, and her tongue flicked out to sweep it away. My dick perked up. Stupid fucking thing. What did it know?

I shoved a fork in my rice and ate, but my appetite had waned in the few minutes since I'd thrown the meal together. I dropped the fork and pushed the plate away.

"Not hungry?" she asked, then without waiting for an answer, she carried on. "I'm here until five. Is there anything in particular you'd like to do?"

"With you?" I snorted. "No."

"Suit yourself." She finished her sandwich and, very precisely, folded the square of aluminum foil she must have wrapped it in, put it in her pocket, then got to her feet. "I think I'll take a walk around your grounds. I need to get today's steps in."

Her proprietary attitude set my jaw. This wasn't how these things usually went. Every other woman Sebastian hired had fawned over me, desperately trying to please me while my responses grew in bitterness and cruelty until they eventually quit.

She set off, skirting the swimming pool then making for the perimeter. My eyes tracked her. I did *not* notice the way her hips swayed with exactly the right amount of femininity or how her ponytail swung from side to side with every step. My mind *did not* throw up an image of wrapping it in my fist and yanking hard as she kneeled on all fours before me, begging for me to fuck her.

My dick is not *hard or uncomfortable, and my balls are not aching for release.*

I dragged my gaze away and marched inside.

Fuck Izabelle Laker.

Fuck Sebastian.

Fuck the terrorist who ripped out my guts.

Fuck them all.

5

Belle

The heavy-footed bus driver slammed on the brakes, and I almost head-butted the seat in front of me. Only my quick reactions saved me from a broken nose. I glowered at him, then gathered my things and stepped onto the sidewalk, tired and cranky after yet another long, fruitless day at Miserable Mansion, as I'd dubbed Upton's Malibu home.

Almost five weeks in and still no breakthrough. If anything, his antipathy toward me had grown, like out-of-control reeds on a riverbank. I couldn't even say it was hatred, more indifference, and that was even harder to cope with. If he yelled at me, at least I'd have something to work with. But the chilly silence was starting to get a little depressing. More than depressing. It was pissing me off.

Even the paycheck that arrived today hadn't lifted my mood, and doubts about my abilities and my staying power had begun to creep in. I'd outlasted the previous 'winner' by three days, but the thought of sticking this out for a year made me want to throw things. Heavy things. Preferable at the insufferable Upton Barrick's goddamn head. But losing my temper would demonstrate he was getting to me, and that was the worst thing I could do. It was imperative I remain calm and show him, through unruffled actions, that his nastiness and cold-shouldered approach didn't bother me in the slightest.

I thumped open the front door, but not even the smell of freshly baked bread raised my spirits. I hung my purse on the coat hook beside the door and stomped into the kitchen where Mom was cooking dinner.

"Goddamn Upton Barrick." I plunked my ass into a chair. "I swear the man is lucky I don't own a gun. Or a shovel. I'd bury the unspeakable grouch if I thought I'd get away with it."

Zak chuckled. "Good day, sister dearest?"

I glared at him, too irritated to allow his geniality to chase away my dour mood. "Seriously, if he shoots one more of his vicious stares at me and then snorts at my suggestions of things he might like to do, I won't be held accountable for my actions."

Mom's eyes hazed over, and she glanced at Zak, then back at me. "It can't be easy for him. If anyone understands, it's you, Belle."

I made a frustrated noise then fell silent.

"Have you told him?" Zak asked.

I shook my head, the sting of guilt bringing on a wince. "And I don't intend to, either."

"Why not?" Zak frowned. "If you let him know that you were supposed to be at the same concert that night, he'd at least know you weren't some interfering busybody who hasn't a clue what he's going through. That you, of all people, understand his pain."

"No," I insisted. "That's not the way I want to handle this."

Zak rubbed the back of his neck. He always did that when he disagreed with me.

"You clearly think that's the wrong way to go about things,"

I said as I got to my feet and filled a glass with tap water. I turned around and leaned against the kitchen counter. "Okay, genius, what would you do?"

Zak's lips twisted to one side, and he rolled his wheelchair away from the table. "Y'know, sis, when you're suffering from a disability, or you're not 'perfect', one of the worst things is other people assuming they know what you need, but never actually asking you, almost as if you're no longer capable of making decisions for yourself. He probably feels aggrieved that his friend has hired you, as well as several others before you. Ignoring you is his way of making himself heard because no one is listening to him."

A slab of concrete landed on my chest. "Is that what you think we did with you?"

"No." He shook his head. "We're not talking about me, or him specifically, but in more general terms. In my experience, the minute you're different in some way from the general public, people treat you differently than everyone else."

I sighed and let my head flop backward. "So, what should I do? I've suggested reading, even offering to read to him, doing crosswords, taking a walk. Maybe even going out for a drive. The other day I asked him if he'd like to help me cook lunch. You know what he did? He picked up the bowl where I'd made a lovely salad and tipped the entire thing in the trash, then walked out without saying a word."

A smirk played about Zak's lips, and I shot him an exasperated glare.

"I might have known you'd find that funny." I snorted. "Men."

"Have you even asked him what he wants to do, Belle?"

"I don't need to ask him. The answer would be for me to resign, and that's the one thing I can't do."

"Tell him that's not 'doing' something. That's quitting, and you're not a quitter."

"Okay, so he says, 'I don't want to do anything'. What then?"

"Then you say 'fine', and you let him do absolutely nothing. But that doesn't mean you have to. Knit, sew, do crosswords. Take a dip in his pool. Bake cakes. Read. Watch TV. Go about your life but just do it at his house. Show him you'll give him the space, but that you're there if he wants you, and you're going nowhere. It might take a while, but in the end, he will come around."

I tugged on my bottom lip, reflecting on Zak's advice. As I lifted my eyes to his, a glimmer of a smile grew into something bigger. "You're a smart-ass."

He blew on the tips of his fingers and rubbed them against his polo shirt. "They say the second born is the smart one."

"Yeah, and the firstborn gets the good looks."

Zak threw back his head and laughed. "Keep dreaming, sis."

Mom rolled her eyes. "You two. Nothing changes."

We drifted into silence to eat—food always shut Zak up thankfully—and when we'd finished and Mom rose to clear away the dinner things, I stopped her, insisting she go and put her feet up.

"Zak can help me," I said, shooting a glare at my twin. "He pretends he's helpless, but we all know he's not."

When the doctors broke the news that Zak would never walk again after… I'd been so swamped with guilt, I'd tiptoed around him as if he were surrounded by eggshells and if I cracked even a single one, I'd break his spirit. Zak, being Zak, soon grew tired of that and told me if I continued, he didn't want to see me anymore. A bit difficult considering we lived in the same house, but his blunt directive woke me up to just how amazing my brother was and how little I deserved him. I'd live with the guilt until my dying breath, but I'd learned to manage it around Zak, and over time, we'd picked our way through the debris of our lives and rediscovered the kind of relationship we had before his spinal cord was severed.

Zak waited until Mom disappeared into the living room, and then he picked up a leftover crust of bread and threw it at me, grinning.

I shook the crumbs from my hair. "Asshole," I said, but I couldn't stop a grin edging across my face. "Remember the food fights we used to have?"

"Do I ever," Zak said. "I also remember the slap to the back of my head when Mom discovered mashed potato smeared all over her kitchen cabinets."

My eyes misted over. "Good times," I said wistfully.

Zak wheeled over, carrying the plates in his lap. He set them next to the sink. "There's better times ahead, sis."

I looked down at him, my vision blurring. "I dreamed about Marin the other night. I miss him, Zak."

Zak squeezed my fingers. "You can't live in the past, Belle. None of us can. Heartbreak lies that way, trust me."

"How do you stay so positive?"

He shot me a crooked smile, the one that made the dimple in his right cheek appear. I had an identical one in my left cheek.

"Life's for living, sis. I could have chosen a different path, one where I spent my days sitting in this thing and hiding away from the world, but I'm twenty-three. I have years ahead of me, and I intend to live my life to the fullest."

"You amaze me."

Zak winked. "I am pretty amazing."

I raised my eyes to the ceiling. "Jerk."

"Talking of jerks, guess who I saw yesterday?"

"Who?"

"Wyatt."

I flattened my lips at the mention of Marin's brother. Wyatt had never liked me. Actually, strike that. Wyatt hated me. He'd told me straight to my face on many occasions that I wasn't good enough for his brother and he'd tried, multiple times, to get Marin to break things off. Jerk was too kind a word for that guy. After Marin died, Wyatt said some awful things that heaped even more guilt on my already bowing shoulders. Things I'd never even told Zak. I'd seen him two or three times since Marin's funeral but had gone out of my way to make sure our paths didn't cross.

"Relax, Belle," Zak said. "He's moving to Florida."

I brightened considerably. The other side of the country might just be far enough away, even though I'd prefer the other side of the world. "Great. Let's hope he stays there."

Zak chuckled. "Thought you might like that slice of news. And on the Upton Barrick thing, try not to worry. You'll figure it out. You always do."

"Yeah, maybe, although you'd probably get through to him far easier than I would. Sebastian Devereaux hired the wrong Laker."

"Nu-uh," Zak replied. "You were gifted the patience genes."

"And the looks." I winked. "Don't forget the looks."

Zak turned on the faucet and flicked water at me. "Whatever."

I squealed and ducked for cover as he continued to spray me with water. "You're dead," I shouted, laughing harder than I had in weeks.

"There's only ever one winner in this game, Belle, and it ain't ever you."

We messed around for a few more seconds until I conceded defeat, and then we tidied the kitchen and wiped up every drop of water. I was surprised Mom hadn't come to break up our play fighting, but when I walked into the living room, she was fast asleep, an open magazine on the floor by her feet.

Yet another reason I had to stick out this job to the very end. Not only was the monthly salary almost double what I made at the retirement home looking after my elderly residents, but the end-of-year bonus would mean Mom could leave one of her jobs.

Whatever Upton Barrick did to try to make me quit, I couldn't let him win.

6

Belle

I powered up the steep incline from the bus stop to Upton's mansion. The weather reporter stated that today was set to be the hottest July on record, and already sweat trickled between my shoulder blades and my breasts.

Following our conversation last night, I'd decided to take Zak's advice and ask Upton if there was anything particular he'd like to do today. If he greeted me with cold silence or a sharp snap of his tongue, I'd leave him to it and do my own thing. Hence the duffle bag slung over my shoulder contained a two-piece swimsuit and a large bottle of sunscreen, as well as a thick book that should keep me occupied all day. If he wanted to play this game, I'd prove to him that I played it better.

Thanks, bro.

I reached the gate and tapped on the keypad. The second the gates began to open, I blew out the breath that I held every single day since I'd arrived. I kept expecting Upton to change the code. I was surprised he hadn't, although if I thought back to what Sebastian said, it sounded as if he'd tried that in the past, and for whatever reason, it hadn't been successful. I didn't know how he'd behaved with the other women hired to keep him company, but with me, he'd definitely adopted the silent approach.

Perhaps he cycled through strategies until he found one that worked. Maybe today would be the day he'd switch to yelling or saying mean things in the hope I'd finally quit. Whatever he did, I had to remain professional and aloof, and not rise to his poor treatment of me. Upton Barrick struck me as the kind of man who wasn't afraid to press buttons and see what happened. You didn't become a billionaire in your twenties if you were afraid of upsetting people. The loss of his sister and the physical challenges he'd faced since the terrorist exploded a bomb that killed ninety-four Angelinos might have knocked him off course, but the backbone he undoubtedly owned was still there, buried beneath his pain.

The house was a fair distance from the road, but I'd gotten used to the daily hike. Better than a gym workout, in my opinion. I breezed into the large hallway, silently thanked the creator of air-conditioning, and headed straight for the kitchen where I'd find Barbara waiting with a cold drink for me. We'd settled into a routine, and she never let me down.

"You're an angel," I said, taking the iced tea from her. I drank deeply. "It's so hot today, and it's still early."

"Yeah, gonna be a record breaker." She bustled over to the fridge and removed a basket of strawberries and raspberries, and a big tub of cream. "Eton Mess for after lunch?"

"Sounds divine." Upton had stopped accusing me of stealing food when I hadn't reacted as I presume he'd intended —with rage or at the very least annoyance.

I dropped my duffel bag in the corner where it wouldn't get in Barbara's way. "Where is he?"

She jerked her head toward the backyard. "He looks tired today."

I nodded. "I'll go say hello. I just love being ignored."

Barbara laughed. "It's a good thing you have patience."

I made a move to leave her to her work, then hesitated and turned back around. "What was he like? Before, I mean."

Barbara straightened, a large silver bowl in her hands. She set it down and then opened the tub of cream and poured it in. "He smiled more."

She fell silent, and I got the distinct impression she thought it somewhat of a betrayal to talk to me about him. It wasn't fair of me to pump her for more information, so I shot her an apologetic grin and went in search of Upton.

Barbara hadn't undersold his apparent tiredness. Dark circles dogged the skin beneath his eyes, and a shadow over his jawline meant he hadn't yet shaved. His hair stuck out at all angles as if he'd been raking it with his fingers, and an untouched cup of coffee sat on the table in front of him.

"Morning," I said brightly, flopping into a chair at a right angle to his. "Boy, it's so hot already."

He kept staring ahead. "Then I suggest you stay inside where it's cool."

The absence of a follow-up request for me to leave fired a spark of hope within me.

"What would you like to do today?"

He turned his head, his gaze steady and cold. "What's this, Izabelle? Psychology one oh one?"

Despite several attempts to encourage him to call me Belle, he'd ignored every single one. I'd given up correcting him.

"I was thinking last night." I refrained from telling him I'd talked to my brother. Partly because I worried he'd take it all wrong and assume I was blabbing about him to anyone who bothered to listen, and partly because I wanted to keep my personal life private. "I realize I've suggested lots of things you might want to do, but I haven't asked you what you want. And I'm sorry. I should have."

He cast me a withering glare, then shifted his gaze back across the expanse of pristine lawn surrounded by tall trees. A pulse ticked in his jaw.

I'd like to put my lips there.

The involuntary—and unwelcome—thought came at me from left field, and a hot flush crept up my neck. Thankfully, he paid me no attention, giving the blush time to subside. Not once in the last five weeks had any inappropriate musings toward this man entered my mind, so why now?

Liar. You think about him all the time.

I rapidly blinked, ready to start an argument with myself—I did that from time to time—when Upton's striking amber eyes landed on mine once more, as cold as a few minutes earlier. Maybe colder.

"What I want, Miss Laker, is for you to fuck off. Clear enough for you?"

He stood, picked up the untouched cup of coffee, poured it into a large planter with a shrub full of crimson flowers that brightened the patio area, and stomped inside.

I heaved a great big sigh.

That went swimmingly.

Then again, I hadn't expected him to do a complete one-eighty, bump fists, and tell me he wanted to be besties.

In a way, I was relieved he'd gone. It gave me a few precious minutes to organize my thoughts and slow my pulse. Upton Barrick was a beautiful man. There, I'd admitted it. The jagged scar that ran the length of his face didn't detract from his exquisite good looks. And those golden eyes... unique, absorbing, filled with pain.

Get a grip, Belle.

The flash of attraction that had emerged from God only knew where had to be squished like a bug hitting a car windshield at the height of summer. I could not, *would not*, develop feelings for this man. My interest began and ended with doing my best to help him find a sliver of happiness, making it through an entire year, and collecting the promised bonus. Right now, though, with forty-seven long weeks stretching ahead, I'd better not bank on the cash injection just yet.

I returned to the kitchen. Barbara grimaced at me, which I took to mean Upton had blown through here after he'd left me outside. I hitched up my right shoulder in an attempt at nonchalance and fished my phone out of my bag. Scrolling to the album marked 'Summer in Baja', I pulled up one of my favorite photos of Marin and me. It was our first vacation together after graduating from high school. He'd washed cars, and I'd worked weekends in our local grocery store all through senior year to save enough money for a long weekend in Baja, California. This was taken on our second day. We'd surfed the early morning waves, and he snagged a photo of us afterward with salty hair and happy faces.

Four years later, he'd gone. Left me forever. My childhood sweetheart, and the only man I'd ever love, and I'd never see him again.

I wrapped my arms around myself and held my breath, waiting for the pain to abate. This, right here, was the reason I'd never allow myself to fall in love again. The pain of loss was too acute.

"Izabelle, are you okay?"

I jerked my head up and met Barbara's worried gaze. "Yeah, I'm fine," I said, eager to reassure her. "Okay, what can I do to help you today?"

She motioned with her hand. "There's barely enough work for one, let alone two. You just go and relax, and I'll call you if I need anything."

I poked my tongue into my cheek. "Maybe I should try again with Upton."

"I'd leave him right now. Let him come around in his own time."

"It's been five weeks, Barbara. I don't think he's going to come around on his own, and I promised Sebastian I'd try."

"Sebastian understands," she said, shaking her head sadly. "More than most. He doesn't expect you to perform miracles. Just..." She broke off, and I could have sworn her eyes filled with tears. She blinked rapidly. "Don't give up on him."

I walked over to her and gave her a hug. "I won't."

"Good. Now go. Sunbathe, read, swim. Make yourself at home."

It felt so wrong to take advantage of the facilities at Upton's home, but my options were pretty limited. My contract stated I was to remain at the house between the hours of nine a.m. to five p.m. Monday through Friday. If Upton wouldn't engage, then what else could I do other than sit around, wait for him to appear from wherever he'd taken himself off to, and try again.

I changed in the pool house and, after testing the warmth of the water with my toe, dove into the deep end. My body instantly cooled. I swam twenty-five lengths, surprised I'd managed that much. I loved to swim but rarely got the opportunity.

Laying a towel on one of the sun loungers that framed the pool, I let the sun dry my skin, but the heat was too oppressive to stay there very long.

I returned to the pool house, changed back into my clothes, and went in search of Barbara to see if I could help with lunch preparation. She set me to work grating cheese for the omelets she planned to make when the doorbell rang. My head snapped up. Upton hadn't received one visitor since I'd started working here, and he'd only left the house once to my knowledge, although I had no idea where he'd gone.

"That'll be Antonio." Barbara rinsed her hands under the

tap. "You wouldn't be a dear and go get him for me, would you?"

"Who's Antonio?" I asked.

"He's the interim CEO of the ROGUES' West Coast operations. He's taking care of things while Upton is... on sabbatical. He comes by every few weeks with an update. Be a love, will you, and show him to Upton's study, and then go find Upton and let him know Antonio's arrived."

"Oh, sure."

I paced through the house to the front door. When I opened it, a man in his fifties with gray hair and twinkling blue eyes greeted me, his white-toothed smile broad and wide.

"Hey. You must be Izabelle. I'm Antonio." He thrust out his hand. "Sebastian told me he'd hired you. How are things?"

There were certain people in this world that set your teeth on edge and gave you the heebie-jeebies, and then there were people like Antonio who instantly put you at ease and caused you to crave their company. I returned his warm, friendly smile with one of my own.

"Call me Belle," I said. "Come on in. It's so hot out there. You must be boiling in that suit."

He waved dismissively. "I'm used to it. So, tell me, how is our resident grump doing?"

I smiled. "Still grumpy."

Antonio chuckled. "It's good that you have a sense of humor. You'll need it."

I wrinkled my nose. "You're not the first to point that out."

He walked alongside me, clearly knowing where he was going. We arrived outside Upton's office, and I gestured for him to go inside. "I'll see if I can find him. Can I get you anything to drink?"

"All good here. Take your time."

I started my search in the living room where Upton occasionally hung out to listen to music, but he wasn't there. Nor was he in the library, and when I checked to see if he'd somehow snuck past me and gone to the kitchen, Barbara said she hadn't seen him either. I peeked through the rear windows in case he'd returned to the pool despite the soaring temperatures, but still no luck.

Damn the man. He must have known to expect Antonio and yet, rude oaf that he was, he'd made himself scarce.

After I'd checked every room on the first floor, I traipsed upstairs to the second floor and padded along the thickly carpeted hallway to Upton's bedroom. This was the only other place he could be. I rapped twice on the door and waited. When he didn't answer, I knocked again, and then, risking his wrath, I pushed open the door. A quick scan around showed me he wasn't in the bedroom, but the sound of running water drew my eyes to his adjoining bathroom.

My breath caught in my throat. The door to the bathroom was wide open, giving me a direct view of the shower stall. The rising steam didn't stop a clear view of Upton, facing away from me.

Oh my God.

His whole back was covered in scars, some faded to silver, others still red and bumpy. My chest tightened, and I couldn't get enough air into my lungs. The pain he must have been in and, given how some of those wounds still looked raw, continued to suffer...

Anger crawled into my throat. I thought I'd doused the flames of fury, or at least tamped them down enough to cope from day to day, but seeing Upton and what he had to face every day brought it all back. The heinous act of the terrorist who'd exploded a bomb at a crowded concert with no thought for the loss of innocent life was something that still haunted me to this day. If that bastard wasn't already dead, I'd fucking kill him myself using only my bare hands.

Breathe, Belle. Slowly. In. Out. In. Out.

My legs trembled, and I put out a hand to steady myself. After a minute of deep breathing, the way I'd been taught, my heart rate slowed and the fit of rage abated.

It occurred to me that despite the heat of this year's summer and access to a private swimming pool, I'd never seen Upton without his shirt on, and now I had, I understood why he wanted to hide his pain beneath his clothing.

My heart cracked a little. Surprising since I'd always believed what happened to Marin had broken it fully and completely.

Standing here in Upton's personal space when he'd made it clear his bedroom was off limits felt all wrong, an imposition. A crime against his privacy.

I slowly backed away.

And then he turned around, and our eyes locked.

Fuck.

7

Upton

Thirty minutes earlier

I left Izabelle *fucking* Laker sitting out on my patio and marched past Barbara, muttering under my breath. Five weeks. Five fucking weeks where I'd hardly even acknowledged her existence, and even when I had deigned to speak to her, I'd kept it brief, cold, and cutting.

And she just kept coming back for more.

Fucking woman.

Just like all the rest, wanting to fix me, to help me, to fucking talk to me when all I wanted was silence. I had enough voices screaming in my head. I didn't need another one carping on from the outside. Her unwanted presence was a source of constant irritation, like a stone in my shoe, one I couldn't get rid of no matter how hard I tried.

There was one thing different about her, though. She was the first one to ask me what I wanted. Only took her five goddamn weeks. Then again, if the others had stuck around as long as she had, maybe they'd have realized how offensive I found it when people made assumptions they weren't entitled to make.

I found myself in the living room and I put on some music which usually soothed me when I got in one of my low moods. Not today. My skin itched, not physically like a rash, but deep down, almost as if the poison of guilt roared through my veins.

Why did you get those fucking tickets?

I'd asked myself the same thing a million times. A pointless question, but one I couldn't stop, no matter how much my therapist told me it wasn't my fault. I'd ended his visits in the end because nothing he said helped, and I came away from every session feeling more desperate and alone than I had before he'd arrived.

I turned off the music and plodded upstairs to take a quick shower. Antonio would be here soon with his regular—and frankly pointless—performance update. Every few weeks, regular as clockwork, he'd turn up all excited about the latest profit statement. I only humored him because Antonio was a nice guy who didn't deserve the cold shoulder, but in reality, I didn't care how ROGUES was performing or what the plans were for the next expansion of the telecoms business, or the hotel chain, or Ryker's baby *Poles Apart*, his stupid string of exotic dance clubs.

I gave up caring when Jenna's heart stopped beating.

As I crossed my bedroom to grab fresh clothes from my closet, I passed by the large picture window that overlooked the backyard. I skidded to a halt, my heart tripping.

Sweet fucking Jesus.

Izabelle sauntered across the patio from the pool house in a sunshine-yellow two-piece that coordinated perfectly with her butterscotch hair tinged with golden highlights. The bikini top pushed her breasts together, giving her a cleavage that ninety-nine-point-nine percent of the heterosexual men on the planet would offer a kidney just to have a chance to bury their face in for five goddamn seconds. My gaze traveled south to her flat stomach and flared hips, and her slim, shapely legs that would look fucking perfect wrapped around my neck.

Shit.

Nope.

I tried to tear my gaze away. Really, I did, but damn, every single time, my eyes snapped back to her like they were attached to a piece of elastic. She tested the water with her toe, then dived in. Her strokes were smooth and true, and she cut through the water with ease.

I lost track of how long I stood there with my feet glued to the carpet, watching her swim. When she raised herself out of the water and walked over to a nearby lounger, then lay down, droplets of water glistening in the sun, I couldn't help it. I unfastened my jeans and shoved my hand inside my boxers. The second I gripped my rock-hard dick, a tortured groan sounded in my throat. I pumped hard and fast, and when she stood and bent over to pick up her towel, giving me the perfect view of her perfect tits, I orgasmed. Thick ropes of semen stained my shirt and coated my stomach, and I didn't care. I didn't give a shit because, man, the tension that had been riding me all morning finally fucked off.

I yanked my shirt over my head and wiped my hands on it, then tossed it into the laundry basket and made a mental note to start a laundry load this afternoon. The last thing I needed was for Barbara to find a polo shirt crusted with sperm. She might've been with me for years, and prior to Jenna's passing, she'd probably seen her fair share of shocking sights given the number of women I used to bring back here. Multitudes of them. Not any longer, though. I hadn't had sex in over a year. Women didn't interest me any longer.

Until now, a voice whispered.

No!

So I'd masturbated while watching an attractive woman sunbathe. Big fucking deal. It didn't mean I found her the slightest bit attractive. I didn't. I'd used her, that's all. Used her for my own sexual gratification. Same as if I'd bought the latest copy of *Penthouse* and jizzed all over the centerfold.

A meaningless orgasm. A necessary physical release for a man my age.

I slipped off my jeans and boxers, entered the bathroom, and flicked on the shower. I'd almost cleaned myself off when a sixth sense made me glance over my shoulder. Standing in the doorway, a look of complete horror on her face, stood Izabelle.

Blind rage flushed through me.

What the fuck is she doing here?

I reached for a towel and slung it around my waist, then turned the water off and stormed into my bedroom.

"Get out," I growled, my voice dangerously low, my scowl enough to scare the toughest of men into retreat, let alone a mere woman. "Get the fuck out of my bedroom, my house, my goddamn life."

Izabelle held her hands up, palms facing me. "I'm sorry. I shouldn't have invaded your privacy."

"No," I bit out. "You shouldn't have. Now get out."

She shook her head. "Not when you're like this. Talk to me, Upton. I can help you if you'll just let me."

I picked up the first thing I laid my hands on. A marble lamp sitting on my nightstand. I threw it.

Not at her.

Maybe at her.

It smashed against the wall to her right, sending jagged

shards reminiscent of the network of scars all over my body falling to the floor. Izabelle ducked, covering her head.

When she straightened, the hurt expression she wore would have given the hardest of souls pause for thought.

Not me, though.

I grabbed another object, a harmless book this time, and launched it in her direction

She caught it like a basketball pro, her hand snatching it from the air.

"Fuck off, Izabelle!" I hollered, expelling all the frustration that had built up over the past five weeks when my cold, silent approach and occasional barbed comment hadn't scared her off. It'd worked with the others. Why not her? "Fuck. Off. Leave me alone. Stop trying to save me. I can't be saved. Just let me be."

"I can't do that," she said gently.

I hung my head, not in shame for my angry outburst, for throwing the lamp and the book. I hung it out of desperation. She had to go. I'd seen the shock on her face from seeing my scars. I didn't blame her. They were hideous. But now, whenever I looked at her, I'd get an action replay of that expression. I'd suffered through a lot of pity over the last year, but somehow, seeing her face flood with sympathy was worse than all the others added together.

"Whatever they're paying you, I'll double it. Triple it. I'll do anything to make you leave."

She twisted her lips to the side. "Bad luck, handsome. Your friends already anticipated that move. I admit, I expected that offer much sooner. You lasted five weeks. Well done."

Handsome? Bullshit. Not any longer. Not with my ruined body and hideously scarred face.

"Did they pay you to lie, too?" I asked, my lip curved in a sneer. "There's nothing handsome about me, angel of mercy.

Not on the outside, and certainly not on the inside. Now do yourself a favor and leave before I really hurt you."

She stared at me for a split second, then spun on her heel and left the room. I sagged in relief. Finally, *fucking finally,* I'd gotten through to her. I should have lost my shit weeks ago, rather than giving her the silent treatment. If I'd known all I had to do was yell at her and throw things, I could've saved myself a whole lot of trouble.

The sound of her footsteps padding downstairs reached me, and I sagged onto my bed, letting my head fall into my hands. If I wanted her to go so badly, and I'd gotten my wish, why did I feel as if I'd suffered a huge and important loss?

The creak of the second-to-top stair reached me, and when I looked up, Izabelle reappeared holding a trash bag and a broom.

A fucking broom.

What. The. Ever-loving. Hell?

"What are you doing?" I gritted out, my jaw clenched so tight, I was at risk of grinding my teeth to dust.

"Cleaning up," she answered as if picking up the shattered remains of a Tiffany lamp was an everyday occurrence. "Unless you want to do it. In fact, you probably should. You caused the mess."

She thrust the wooden broom handle at me and dropped the trash bag at my feet. I stared at her, unmoving.

"No? Didn't think so."

She bent down to pick up the bag. My eyes locked on to the valley beneath her cleavage, and my dick jerked beneath the towel.

I sprang upright and snatched the bag from her hands, tossing it over her shoulder. "Leave the goddamn lamp. Just get out."

She crossed her arms, a look of fierce determination on her face. "I will. As soon as you apologize."

I widened my eyes. "What?"

"Apologize. For yelling. For throwing the lamp. For being an all-round grouse. Say you're sorry and I'll go."

A rush of adrenaline fueled my blood, and I acted without thinking. My fingers gripped her chin, and I smashed my mouth on hers, forcing her lips apart with my tongue. Need for her, urgent, desperate, new, swamped me, and I reveled in the loss of control.

Seconds passed, and I realized she hadn't moved. Like a block of stone, she stood there, arms hanging loosely by her sides, letting me kiss her but refusing to participate, to kiss me back. I released her as fast as I'd come on to her and took several steps back. Heat rushed to my face, and I dropped my gaze.

Knee deep in silence, I eventually tilted up my chin to find her green eyes trained on me. I tried to get a read on her feelings. She greeted me with a blank stare.

"You have a visitor," she finally said. "I'll let him know that you'll be with him in a few minutes." She turned to walk away, then stopped and came around to face me once more.

"If kissing me was your attempt to force me to leave, Upton, then I'm sorry to disappoint you. But let me make one thing crystal clear. If you touch me again without my permission, you will find yourself slapped with a sexual harassment suit."

With her back erect, she walked to the door, closing it quietly behind her. No anger. No drama. Just pure class.

Shit.

8

Belle

I made it as far as the library before my legs gave out. I covered my face with my hands as I collapsed into the plush leather sofa. Upton kissed me. *He kissed me.* The sheer effort it had taken not to wrap my fingers in the tendrils of his damp hair at the nape of his neck and plaster myself to his taut, firm chest sapped every ounce of energy I had. His lips were hard and demanding, and the way his tongue stroked mine...

If I'd believed for one second he'd kissed me because he wanted to, I wouldn't have held back. But he hadn't wanted to kiss me at all. I'd pissed him off with my refusal to leave, to obey his barked-out orders, to bend to his will. The kiss had been his final shot at getting me to go, to leave him alone, and if I'd relented and kissed him back, he'd have won the war.

I refused to let him win. Not today. Not tomorrow. Not ever. All he'd achieved by kissing me was to make me even more determined to stick this contract out to the bitter end.

My fingers hovered over my lips, and I touched them and

let my eyes fall shut. More than a year had passed since I'd felt a man's lips on my own. I'd loved Marin, heart and soul, but he'd never kissed me in rage, and I hadn't expected to find it such a turn-on. Marin always treated me like a china doll, one he must revere and take care of. He always put my needs first, never his own, and not once in the six years we were together had he ever raised his voice in anger.

Upton's ferocious kiss and the way he'd entered my mouth using brute force, taking no prisoners and asking for no apologies, had aroused feelings in me I'd never experienced. If he could make me this wet with one kiss, then what could he do if I allowed him to go further?

Wait. What are you talking about?

Why would I want to allow Upton Barrick to touch me again? My heart broke when I buried Marin, smashed to smithereens. Unfixable. I wanted to help Upton, not screw him. I still hoped that fixing him might just be the catalyst to help me move on with my own life. A sort of retribution, of paying a debt that could never be fully settled, but if I could help Upton get past all this, I might at least make some inroads into making peace with myself.

Deciding that I'd pulled myself together enough to show my face in public, I went to tell Antonio that Upton would be along shortly. As I exited the library, I shot a quick glance up the stairs in case Upton was a fast dresser and already on his way down. Fortunately for me, he wasn't.

After speaking with Antonio, I headed for the kitchen, but when I found it empty, I grabbed my bag and wandered outside and took a seat in the shade. Might as well read for a little while. It wasn't like there was anything else to do.

My grumbling stomach sent me inside shortly after, and this time, Barbara was there, standing over the stove stirring a pot of something that smelled divine. I peered over her shoulder and sniffed.

"You're a culinary marvel," I said. "What is it?"

"Prawn jambalaya." She held up a spoon, her hand underneath to catch any drips, and held it toward me. "Here, taste."

I blew on the food, then closed my mouth around the spoon. "Oh, that's yummy."

"I made enough for you to take home. I'm sure your mama would appreciate a night off."

I hugged her. "Thank you, Barbara. I'm sure she would."

"Stealing my food again, Miss Laker," a gravelly voice behind me said.

My gaze went to the entranceway to find Upton standing there with his arms folded across his chest, his shoulder propped against the doorjamb. I searched his face to read his mood, but his expression gave nothing away.

"Barbara, can you see Antonio out, please? He's in my study packing up his things."

"I can do it," I offered. Anything to escape Upton's blank stare.

"No. You stay exactly where you are, Miss Laker."

Barbara shot me one of her 'Oh no. What's wrong now?' looks, then scuttled off.

As soon as she was out of earshot, Upton strolled into the kitchen. He bent over the stove and smelled the jambalaya. "She's a great cook."

"I agree," I said. "I didn't ask her for the food. She offered. But if it offends you that much, I'll decline."

He turned around and leaned back, crossing one foot over the other at the ankle. "I'm sorry."

My eyebrows shot north, and my mouth popped open by at least an inch. "For what?" I eventually asked.

He raked his fingers through his hair, and I guessed it must still be damp from the shower when it stuck up at all angles. He'd never looked more stunning with his amber-gold eyes and five o'clock shadow, and the square jaw that often locked with irritation whenever I was in the vicinity.

Jesus, Belle. Quit it, okay.

"I shouldn't have thrown the lamp, and I shouldn't have kissed you. It won't happen again."

My gut lurched. Why did that promise never to touch me again make me feel as if I'd lost something when it wasn't mine in the first place?

"You were mad."

He nodded. "I still am."

"At me?"

He breathed out heavily, and his eyes filled with despair. "At the world."

Almost as if there was an invisible tether between us, and Upton tugged on it, I advanced toward him, my feet moving without my approval. I had to tip my head back to look up at him, despite his slouched position against the counter. "I know you won't believe me when I say this, but I do understand. I'm not the enemy, Upton, whatever you might think. If you ever change your mind and decide you might like a friend to offload on..." I did a pretend curtsey. "I'm your girl."

His lips twitched at the corners, the first sign I'd seen that I might have a chance of reaching him. He pushed himself upright, and I held my breath, wondering what his next move might be.

If I'm not interested, why is my heart racing and why are my fingers itching to run through his hair?

"Take all the food you like. Barbara always cooks too much anyway."

He brushed past me and left.

Saturday morning dawned bright and clear and, finally, the soaring temperatures had fallen to more manageable levels. I rolled over in bed, stretched, then got up. I looked forward to every weekend—not least because it gave me respite from Upton. After our mini breakthrough in the kitchen, I'd thought he was thawing, at least a little. Instead, these past few days, he'd retreated back into his shell, although when he did emerge and our paths crossed, his comments weren't quite as cutting.

This weekend, however, was more special than normal. A friend of mine ran an animal rescue shelter, and occasionally she asked me to help out when holiday season hit or staff were off sick. She'd called me on Thursday to ask if I had time to go down this weekend and walk some of the dogs for her. I'd jumped at the chance of doing something worthwhile and hopefully take my mind off Upton. These days, I thought about him a lot.

Too much.

Especially the kiss.

And that chest, and those abs. And his broad, muscular shoulders leading to defined deltoids and arms strong enough to protect any woman.

Guilt roared through me. I had no business thinking about another man. I still loved Marin. I'd always love Marin, and somehow, it felt as if I was betraying him by fantasizing about Upton.

I shook my head of unwelcome thoughts, showered and dressed in record time and, pinching a slice of Zak's toast—much to his chagrin—I set off for the bus stop.

A half hour later, I disembarked, then made the ten-minute walk from where I'd gotten off the bus to the animal shelter. I headed straight for the tiny office and entered. Ariadne sat behind a battered old desk surrounded by paperwork, tins of cat food, and boxes of dog treats. Piled high all around were bags of feed donated by kind souls who loved animals as much as I did.

"Your angel of mercy has arrived," I announced.

"Thank God," she said, clambering to her feet. She hugged me, and I plucked a stalk of straw out of her hair. "You're a lifesaver."

"What's first?" I asked.

"The dogs need feeding. I've tried to do it like ten times and failed. The phone keeps ringing, which is good, but doesn't help at feeding time."

"Leave it with me."

I fed the dogs, both pleased to see that none of them were the same as the last time I was here, which meant people were adopting them, but simultaneously, it saddened me to think how many pets were still abandoned every single day. As many as Ariadne re-homed, more lined up for a chance at their forever home.

"Okay, done," I said. "What's next?"

Ariadne spun around in her chair, her face red with rage. Sitting in her lap was a tiny puppy, no more than a few weeks old. He/she was far too thin, and a horrible green pus oozed from the corner of its right eye.

"Some bastard just left this puppy tied up outside. If hubs hadn't stopped by on his way to work to drop off the sandwich I left on the kitchen counter this morning, the poor little thing might've died of heatstroke before anyone found him."

"Who would do such a thing?" I exclaimed, reaching down to pluck the soft bundle from her arms. I checked out the undercarriage. A boy. Tucking him into the crook of my arm, I tickled his tummy, and he yawned, then emitted a contented whimper.

"I don't know," she said, her teeth gnashing together. "But they'd better hope I never catch up to them. Why the hell didn't they just bring him inside?"

I shrugged. "Who knows? Maybe they thought they'd be judged or forced into donating. Or maybe they're just cruel bastards."

She heaved a sigh. "I'd better get ahold of the vet. That infection looks nasty, and if it isn't treated, he could go blind."

Ariadne called the vet while I made some puppy milk. With no idea of his age, I didn't want to risk giving him solid food. For all I knew, he might not have been weaned yet. He wolfed it down. God, he must be starving. I suppressed the urge to make more. If he hadn't been fed properly, giving him too much all at once could make him sick. I'd wait for the vet's assessment first.

Luckily, Ariadne had a good relationship with her vet, and she arrived within thirty minutes. She examined our new resident, declared that he couldn't be older than five or six weeks—far too young not to still be with his mother—and that although the eye infection was nasty, a course of antibiotics should clear it right up. She gave him a shot just to get started, as well as the normal injections puppies needed to ward off infection, and promised to return in a couple of days to check up on him.

With the vet's blessing, I fed him again, and after he finished, he promptly fell asleep in my arms. As I watched his tummy rise and fall with every breath, an idea formed in my mind, one that, as much as I strived to ignore it, kept coming back. I'd tried everything to bring Upton out of himself and failed on every occasion. But a puppy... whose heart wouldn't melt when faced with this level of cuteness? Plus, if Upton had something else to think about, a living, breathing thing that relied on him for its very survival, he might just come to realize there was life after loss.

"When do you think he'll be well enough to go to a new owner?" I asked.

Ariadne put down her pen and rested her hands on her stomach. "Hopefully a couple of weeks. As soon as he puts on some weight. Thankfully, if they get the right care, they bounce back quickly at his age."

I rubbed my lips together. "What would you say if I took him?"

Her eyebrows shot up, wrinkling her forehead. "You'd do that?"

"Well, not me, exactly." I explained about Upton and the lack of progress I'd made. "I think this little pup could be exactly what he needs."

Ariadne canted her head to the side. "I'm not sure, hon. You know as well as I do that getting a puppy for anyone as a surprise isn't a good idea."

"Under normal circumstances I'd agree, but I have a feeling about this. Plus, I'll be there Monday through Friday. If it doesn't work out, then I promise I'll personally re-home him, and I'll foster him until that happens." I hit her with a beseeching grin. "Please."

She nibbled on her lip while she considered my plea. And then she nodded.

"Okay, but the responsibility for that pup's wellbeing is on you."

I grinned. "A task I'll happily accept."

9

UPTON

I paced along the second-floor hallway, shooting the occasional glance over the railings that gave me a perfect view of the front door. Izabelle was running late. In the almost two months she'd worked here, she hadn't turned up for work late once. What if the bus had crashed? I'd seen the way some of those bus drivers negotiated the winding roads along the coast. They drove like total idiots at times.

Over the last three weeks, I'd worked even harder to avoid her. Every time I saw her, my mind went straight back to the kiss. The feel of her lips beneath mine, the way her tits had flattened against my chest, the sound of her breath catching in her throat. Even her lack of reaction didn't stop me from reliving every single moment and wishing things were different.

I couldn't blame her for finding me repulsive. The deep, jagged scar running down my face was the least of the hideous scars I carried, both inside and out. If truth be told, the ones on the inside were even more repellent, hence my determination to keep people at bay. If I opened myself up, then I risked judgement, and I was only just holding things together as it was. All it would take was one person to agree that Jenna's death was my fault, and it'd tip me over the edge. Better to stay apart, aloof, cut off from society in general than risk the opinion of others.

The front door opened, and Izabelle appeared. I reached out a hand to steady myself. *Thank God.*

Wait. What was she holding?

I leaned over the banister to get a closer look.

Izabelle tipped back her head, and her jade-green eyes locked on mine. And then she hit me with a broad smile that flipped my stomach and sent a rush of warmth through my chest.

"Hi," she called up to me. "I brought you something."

She dropped to a crouch and... set down a puppy.

A fucking puppy.

It scampered across the hallway, slipping and sliding on the marble floor. And then, right in the middle, it stopped and...

"Jesus Christ, Izabelle. It's taking a piss on my floor."

She gave me an impish grin and shrugged. "It'll clean. Come meet him."

"No dogs," I stated, more than a little pissed she hadn't even thought to ask whether she could bring her puppy to work with her. "You'll have to take him back to your house."

"Oh, he's not mine," she announced. "He's yours."

Shock pulsed through my body, and I shook my head violently. "No."

"Yes," she said, pulling a pack of tissues from her purse. She mopped up the spillage, put the piss-soaked tissues in a plastic bag and tied a knot in it, then scooped the pup into her arms. "Come down and meet your new friend."

A growl rumbled in my chest. "Take it back, Izabelle."

"Him, not it. And once again, that's a no."

She sauntered off in the direction of my kitchen with the... thing... and disappeared from view. I clenched the railings, my knuckles turning white. What was this... charade? She'd overstepped the mark this time. I could just about put up with her myriad attempts to show me that life was worth living—side note: I disagreed—but this... what was that English phrase that Sebastian loved to use? Oh, yeah, this took the fucking biscuit.

In other words, she had some goddamn nerve.

A dog was a ten-year commitment, at least. Who the *hell* did she think she was?

I stomped downstairs, my feet landing on the carpeted stairs so heavily, I almost dislocated a hip. I caught up with her in the kitchen where she and Barbara were cooing and making those stupid noises women seemed to keep especially for babies and young animals.

"It is not staying here," I reiterated for the avoidance of doubt. "You had no right, Izabelle. This is a major imposition, and one that is definitely outside of your boundaries. Now wherever you got it from, take it back."

"A friend of mine runs an animal shelter. Some cruel person left him tied up outside. He was starving, had a horrible eye infection, and was far too young to be without his mother. That was three weeks ago." She held him toward me. "What if he's re-homed and those people are cruel to him? Could you live with that?"

My jaw worked, and a nerve beat in my cheek like it always did when the familiar stir of anger simmered inside.

"You had no right," I repeated. "And how *dare* you try to heap guilt upon me? Don't you think I carry enough of that around with me as it is?"

I didn't wait for an answer. I spun on my heel and marched out of the kitchen, my long strides bringing me to my study in a matter of seconds. As I drew to a halt, I heard it. A clipping noise. The sound of a dog's claws.

As I turned around, a set of big brown eyes met mine. He plopped his rump on the tiled floor and gazed up at me, then tilted his head to the side, almost as if he was trying to work me out.

Good luck with that.

I had to concede he was quite cute. Tan and white, a patch over one eye, and he had one ear up and one ear down. But still too much trouble. If I'd wanted a dog, I'd have chosen one for myself, not had one foisted on me by an overeager do-gooder who, despite my best efforts, kept coming back for more punishment.

"If you piss on my floor, you are straight back to the pound, do you hear me?"

He whined and then lay down and proceeded to lick his paws.

I rolled my eyes and sat behind my desk, then fired up my computer, hardly even aware of what I was doing until I found myself browsing an online pet store, and the next thing I knew, I had a basket full of puppy gear.

Well, seeing as Izabelle refused to take him back, I guessed he was staying. For now. I still hadn't fully decided. It depended on how much of my stuff he wrecked with his acid piss and penchant to chew everything in sight. Puppies chewed, right? Yeah, maybe add in a few more of those soft rubber rings that the store guaranteed meant your Italian leather shoes remained intact.

I glanced over at the doorway, and a jolt of panic sent me to my feet. Where was it? I mean him. Where was he?

The sound of soft snoring reached me, and I ducked my head beneath my desk. He'd curled up at my feet and I hadn't noticed. I sat on the floor and rubbed behind his ear. Goddammit. Stupid puppy was determined to win me over.

"Long way to go yet, you little fucker."

"Aww, look at you two. Best friends already."

I twisted my head and glowered at Izabelle standing a few feet away. "The jury is out on whether he's staying."

"Sure, it is," she said, a smile tugging at the corners of her mouth. "I'm nipping to the store to pick up a few things for him. Paolo is going to drive me."

"No need," I declared. "I already ordered everything he needs. There's a delivery coming this afternoon."

Her smile widened, and she clutched a hand to her chest. "See, you're not all bad."

"Don't you believe it," I muttered.

"What have you decided to call him?"

I frowned. "Didn't he come with a name?"

"Yeah, not so much. The evil bastards who left him tied up outside the shelter in the searing heat didn't bother to leave a nametag. So, what's it to be?"

I returned my attention back to the sleeping puppy. "Bandit."

She inclined her head. "Bandit it is. I like it."

"You still shouldn't have done it." I locked my eyes on hers. "And I'm not committing to anything."

She rubbed her lips together, forcing me to swallow a groan. Whenever she did that, I had to quell an urge to kiss her. The memory of her lips, still and unmoving beneath mine, appeared in far too many dreams for my liking.

"Fair enough," she said. "But my instincts tell me you two will be inseparable by the end of the week."

~

"Bandit, get the fuck off my bed."

Two weeks had passed, and no matter what I tried, the damn dog was determined to sleep with me. Every night, I'd place him in his basket at the foot of my bed and then turn in, and every morning, I'd wake to find him curled up beside me, his head on the pillow and his paws tucked up to his chin, the picture of fake innocence. Cute, yes, but not the plan.

The original plan had been for him to sleep in the kitchen, but three days of straight howling had seen me cave. I needed sleep more than I needed to train the dog, and so I'd made the kind of rookie mistake lots of new dog owners made—I'd allowed him into my room, and now the little fucker thought he owned the joint.

He lazily opened his eyes, snuffled into the pillow, stretched, then burrowed further into my Egyptian cotton three thousand thread count sheets.

"Little bastard," I groused, throwing back the covers. I tugged on a pair of shorts and a T-shirt and took him downstairs and into the yard. We'd made progress with the toilet training, but I couldn't deny one or two accidents, including a particularly delightful gift one night when I'd woken, thirsty, and decided not to switch the light on to go fetch a drink.

Yeah, I wouldn't make that mistake a second time.

I waited until he'd done his business, then fed him and left him in the kitchen while I showered. When I returned downstairs, Izabelle had arrived, and she was sitting on the kitchen floor tickling Bandit's stomach. A weird feeling filled my chest, a kind of heat accompanied by a heavy weight that made it hard to take a full breath.

"Hey," I rasped.

Her head came up, and her smile made my insides clench. "Hey yourself. Did you manage okay this weekend without me?"

I grunted, picked up the coffeepot, and poured a cup.

"Says it all," Izabelle said. "I knew he'd win you over."

"I didn't say he had."

"You didn't have to."

I glared at her and stomped outside, and Bandit immediately leaped to his feet and trotted out after me like the fucking shadow he'd turned into. Izabelle's chuckles reached me, and I growled.

Goddamn dog.

I sat in the shade and, as if he had springs in his legs, Bandit jumped right into my lap and gave me those big brown eyes that resulted in me scratching him behind the ear as I'd learned he loved.

"Aww, would you look at that," Izabelle said, joining us without invitation. She blew on her fingers and rubbed them against her lapel. "It's so satisfying being right."

I gave her a filthy glower, then returned my attention to the bundle of fluff gazing up at me with complete adoration.

"I need to take him to the vet today," Izabelle continued when I refused to rise to her teasing.

A jolt of panic widened my eyes. "Why? What's wrong with him?"

Her grin almost split her face in two. "Nothing's wrong with him. He's due for a checkup, that's all."

"Oh." I breathed deeply to calm my racing pulse.

She got to her feet. "Well, shall we go?"

As I caught on to her meaning, I shook my head. "You take him."

"No. He's your dog."

"Not by choice," I groused.

"Suck it up, Upton. I'll come along for the ride, but you're taking him."

"Tell the vet to come here."

"They don't make house visits unless it's an emergency."

"Fuck my life," I muttered. "Fine. What time's the appointment?"

"In an hour. We'd best get moving. You never know how bad the traffic might be."

I huffed. "And you couldn't have told me this last week? What if I'm busy?"

She gave me one of her looks, the one that silently screamed 'bullshit'.

"One, I avoided telling you so you couldn't think up some crappy excuse to avoid leaving the house, and two, you and I both know you're not busy. After two and a half months, I think I know your schedule by now—it's virtually nonexistent."

Since when did she get so fucking comfortable ticking me off?

"You're overstepping the mark, Izabelle," I warned. "Know your fucking place."

Irritation propelled me from the chair and forced Bandit to scramble from my lap. Luckily, he had good reflexes and landed like a cat. I paced inside, snatched up Bandit's lead, and by the time I turned around, there he was, right behind me.

"Sit," I ordered.

He obeyed.

"Finally, we're getting somewhere," I mumbled, dropping to a crouch to affix the lead to his collar. By the time I straightened, Izabelle had caught up. I expected a contrite expression; I got a defiant one.

"Ready?" I snapped.

"Yes," she said, and I caught a slight upturn at the corners of her lips.

Damn frustrating woman.

Bandit's claws clicked on the marble floor as we headed for the front door. Outside, I stopped to let him do his business, then scooped him into my arms. I pressed the fob for the garage door, and it opened.

"Five cars!" Izabelle exclaimed from over my shoulder. "Why on earth do you need five cars?"

She drew alongside me, and I glowered at her. "For a recluse, you mean?"

She rolled her eyes. "No, but go ahead and think the worst. I meant who needs five cars, whatever their personal circumstances. You can only drive one at a time."

I rubbed the back of my neck. "I like cars, or at least I used to. Don't drive very much these days."

"No shit," she said, firing a grin in my direction that I refused to rise to.

I lifted the keys to the SUV from a rack hanging by the door and unlocked it.

Izabelle climbed in the front, and I handed Bandit to her. "I guess I need a harness."

She nodded. "We can stop at the pet store on the way home and pick one up."

My insides warmed at the way she'd said "home". Somehow, over the last couple of months, Izabelle had grown from an irritant that I desperately wanted to eject from my life to someone I hungered to see every morning, and mourned when she left at the end of the day. I'd never tell her, of course, because nothing good would come of it. Besides, after the pain of losing my sister, I wouldn't risk putting myself through the pain of loss ever again. Love hurt, and I'd go to the ends of the earth to avoid having my heart ripped out for a second time. Better to cut myself off. Loneliness I could cope with.

I cast a sideways glance at Bandit curled up in Izabelle's arms. A dog I could cope with losing. Just. And I couldn't deny he provided me with companionship. I'd even laughed a few times since Izabelle dumped him on me.

Being on the road felt strange. Apart from regular visits to my plastic surgeon to discuss the ongoing treatment for my shrapnel injuries, I rarely left the sanctuary of home. This would be one of the few times I'd gone anywhere other than the hospital since Jenna's funeral.

A vise closed around my heart, and I winced, but Izabelle didn't notice, her focus on Bandit as she twisted his ear around her finger.

"Are you aware that the running costs on just one of your cars would pay for dog food at the sanctuary for a month?"

I briefly looked at her, then returned my attention to the road. "I meant to talk to you about that. I'd like to make a donation. Who do I call to make that happen?"

As I shot her another glance, her eyes softened, and she smiled. "Ariadne Mills. She runs the place. I'll text you her phone number. Anything you can give would help massively. Fundraising is a never-ending activity, unfortunately. There's always too many abandoned animals and not enough money to care for them."

I nodded, then fell into silence, but it wasn't awkward, or something I desperately wanted to get away from. Driving along PCH with Izabelle sitting beside me, and Bandit curled in her lap, I realized the tension that gnawed at my gut had lessened. Still there, but instead of a raw, visceral, torturous agony, it had waned into a dull ache.

I'm trying, Jenna. I'm really fucking trying.

10

Belle

I answered Ariadne's call, anticipating a request to come by this weekend to help out. Instead, she asked, "Are you fucking that guy?"

My jaw flopped about a bit, and then I squeaked out a response. "What guy?"

"The one you gifted the puppy to."

"No!" I exclaimed. "Jesus, Ariadne, what makes you ask such a thing?"

"Because he just called me and donated a hundred grand."

My chin hit the floor. "He what?" I whispered. "A hundred thousand dollars?"

"Yes."

"Oh my God," I said, thinking back to what I'd said yesterday about how many cars he owned. "I made a comment to him about his wealth, but I didn't expect him to do that as a result."

I heard a snuffle, and then a sob. "You know what this means, Belle."

"Yes," I said, my own tears arriving. "It secures the future of the sanctuary for the next two years."

"Exactly. Tell him thank you for me." She hiccupped. "He kind of caught me off guard, and I'm not sure I thanked him. In fact, I'm almost certain I didn't."

"I will." I sniffed and dabbed at my nose with a tissue. "I'm leaving for work in a few minutes. I'll be sure to tell him."

I hung up and wandered into the kitchen in a kind of daze. I put salt in my coffee instead of sugar, only realizing my mistake after I'd taken a mouthful and spat it into the sink.

Zak appeared at that precise moment. "I agree. I always want to spit out coffee when you make it, too."

I made a face at him and rinsed out my cup, then made a fresh one. "Upton just donated a hundred Gs to the animal sanctuary."

Zak's eyebrows shot up. "Fuck me."

I nodded. "My thoughts exactly."

"Jeez, sis, you must have done something right."

"It's not me, it's Bandit. I knew he'd fall in love with that puppy, given the chance." A smile formed on my lips as I thought of the two of them together. "He's a good man, deep down. He's hurting, that's all."

"Don't underestimate your influence," Zak said, giving me a rare compliment. He usually preferred insults. It was the way we'd rolled our entire lives. "Credit where it's earned."

"You're only being nice to me because your electric wheelchair is due at the store this weekend."

When my second paycheck came through at the beginning of last week, it meant I had enough money put aside to afford a super-duper top-of-the-range chair for Zak. He'd vehemently refused until I'd taken him to the store and let him try them out. Then, he'd had to concede that it would make his life easier, and he'd capitulated.

"That's true," he said, nodding.

I laughed. "Jackass."

The unplanned call with Ariadne, and then updating Zak left me running late, and I had to sprint for the bus, only just making it in time. I sank into my seat, out of breath, hair an unholy mess. I smoothed it with my hands, then settled back for the ride to Upton's home. I virtually skipped up the long driveway, unable to remove the smile plastered on my face. He was changing. He might not see it, but I did. Despite what Zak said, I gave most of the credit to Bandit, but then again, getting Upton a puppy had been my idea, and it seemed to have paid off.

Humming to myself, I entered the house and made my way to the kitchen. I'd usually find Upton there or outside by the swimming pool playing tug with Bandit, or watching the little pup race around, a faint smile curving his lips upward. Today was no different, and I stood by the back door watching him. I liked these moments when he didn't know I was there. It allowed me to see him at his most vulnerable.

He brushed a hand down the back of his head, and his T-shirt rose, exposing a sliver of toned skin. A deepening ache filled my chest, and my stomach tightened. I *was* attracted to Upton, and if he ever kissed me again, I wouldn't hold back. Not this time. But since that one occasion when, despite his denials, he'd kissed me in the hope I'd quit, he'd shown no interest in me whatsoever. At least he didn't grunt at me these days. Well, not too much, anyway.

I stepped onto the patio. "Hi."

He turned his head, and I held my breath, waiting for the scowl. Instead, he smiled. A real smile, not the fake one I'd seen him bestow more times than I cared to count.

"Hey," he said. "Come watch this."

He bent to pick up a ball at his feet and tossed it a fair way. "Bandit, fetch."

A tan-and-white blur raced across the lawn, returning with the ball. He plopped it at Upton's feet and sat, his tongue lolling out the side of his mouth. Upton shot me a triumphant grin.

"You can call me the dog whisperer," he said, laughing.

Oh God. His laugh. I'd give a kidney to hear that again.

He threw the ball, and Bandit took off again. I closed the space between us, stood right in front of him, raised myself up on tiptoes, and kissed his cheek. The scarred one. I chose that side on purpose. Whatever Upton thought, I didn't care about his scars. I cared about him.

He flinched a little, and then he pressed his fingertips to the spot where I'd kissed him. "What's that for?"

"Ariadne called me. You have no idea the difference that will make to her and all the animals she cares for."

"Oh, that." He shrugged it off. "It's nothing."

"Nothing?" I shook my head. "It's an insane amount of money that is going to do so much good, Upton. Thank you. From the bottom of my heart. Ariadne wanted me to make sure I told you thank you from her, too. I think she was too stunned to say it herself."

"No problem." He bent to throw the ball for Bandit again, who'd patiently waited at his feet. "It's no use to me."

"That doesn't change the generosity, at least in my opinion."

"Then you're welcome." He took a seat and gestured for me to do the same. "I need a favor."

"Oh?"

"Yeah." He fiddled with the hem of his T-shirt, his eyes cast downward. "I need you to take Bandit for a few days."

"Why?"

He rubbed his fingertips over his lips and breathed out

heavily. “I have to go into the hospital for an operation. Tomorrow.”

Fear lodged in my throat, a huge lump I couldn’t swallow past. *Please don’t let him be ill.* “What operation?”

He rolled back his shoulders and then cricked his neck. “There’s a piece of shrapnel they need to remove.” He moved his gaze, staring off into the distance where Bandit was digging a hole, lumps of soil flying into the air from his efforts. “It’s shifted, enough for my surgeon to want to take it out. It was supposed to be in a few weeks, but following the results of my last scan, he decided to bring the appointment forward. Hence the last-minute request.”

My chest ached, and my vision blurred. I blinked several times, grateful that Upton’s attention was elsewhere. If I’d learned anything about him it was that he abhorred pity. And I didn’t pity him. I hurt for him. I wished I could take his pain and mine and bury it inside that hole Bandit had dug.

“How long will you be in the hospital for?”

“Couple of days. But I’ll be a bit stiff afterward, and having him leap on me as he regularly does isn’t ideal.”

He met my gaze then. Thankfully, my eyes were clear, and I schooled my expression.

“I have a better idea,” I said. “I’ll come to stay. That way, Bandit isn’t ripped from his home at a time he’s still settling in, and I can be on hand in case you need anything.”

“No.”

His rebuttal came instantly, and it irritated me. I squared my shoulders, readying myself for battle.

“Yes,” I hit back. “It isn’t fair to Bandit. He’ll only get confused.”

“You are not staying here.”

“Why? What are you so afraid of?” I asked.

His face bloomed with color, his eyes cold and hard, the way they used to be when I first arrived. “Fuck you, Izabelle. I’m not afraid of anything. I just don't want you here. You foisted the damned dog on me. You fix this."

He launched to his feet so fast, his chair keeled over. He left it where it lay and stomped inside the house, Bandit speeding after him, his little legs a blur as he ran to be by his master's side. I let out a deep sigh. He didn't fool me. Upton's fear was allowing me to witness his pain, his suffering, to see him in a weakened state. He was a proud man, and despite his reclusive nature, he wanted to be seen as strong and in control. Laid up in bed after an operation with me fluffing his pillows was right up there with his worst nightmare.

Well, too bad. Barbara had her own family to take care of, and Paolo wouldn't be any use. A nice guy, but not exactly nursemaid material. Mom and Zak would be fine for a few days. Upton wouldn't. He needed me, and dammit, he'd have to suck it up.

Zak's warning about taking over and ignoring what Upton wanted came back to me, but on this occasion, I disagreed with his assessment. Upton was letting his stubbornness get in the way, and a back operation wasn't anything to take lightly.

I went into the house and found him sitting in the living room, his eyes closed, Bandit on his lap, and rock music blasting from the speakers. I turned off the music.

His eyes snapped open. "I was listening to that," he bit out.

"And you can listen to it again in a moment—after you've damn well listened to me. Here are your choices. I'm staying over for a few days. Or I quit."

The words came out before I'd properly thought them through, and if he accepted, I was well and truly screwed. But something... I don't know... an instinct told me he wouldn't accept my resignation. Not anymore. He liked having me around, not that he'd ever admit it.

He set Bandit on the couch beside him and got to his feet.

Three steps brought him right in front of me. His jaw ticked dangerously, but I refused to budge.

"You won't quit. You need this fucking job too much."

"Not enough to pander to your childish antics, I don't."

"My childish..."

He broke off, annoyance swimming in his amber eyes. And then he muttered, "Fuck it."

He moved fast, his large hand clasping the back of my neck, and he yanked me into his hard body. His mouth crashed down on mine, his tongue demanding entry. Unlike last time when I'd sapped every ounce of energy in order to resist him, on this occasion, I capitulated. I wound my arms around his neck and opened my mouth beneath his. A groan rumbled through his chest, and the sound weakened my knees. I sank a couple of inches, and his strong arms held me in place.

Damn, the man could kiss. Butterflies swamped my stomach, and a heavy ache settled between my legs. He cupped my ass, tugging me closer. His thick erection bumped against my belly.

Oh God. More.

He tore away, his chest heaving, a mirror image of mine. I licked my lips, then rubbed my fingertips over them. Both of us stared at each other in silence, neither able to muster the right words.

Upton broke first. "Still sure you want to come to stay, Izabelle?"

"Yes," I rasped, my voice thick with desire.

"Really?" he questioned. "Because I can't guarantee that's the last time I'll kiss you. I opened the door, but you allowed me to walk through it when you could have—should have—slammed it shut."

His words sent a tremor racing up my spine. He was warning me off while at the same time reeling me in. Giving me an exit strategy while letting me know what would happen if I chose not to take it.

I locked my eyes on his. "Yes," I reiterated.

His eyes gleamed with a mixture of triumph and trepidation. "I'll ask Barbara to make up one of the spare rooms."

And then he brushed past me with Bandit hot on his heels, leaving me alone with my thoughts.

11

Belle

"The house feels weird without Upton here," I said, flopping into a chair at the kitchen table while Barbara kneaded freshly made dough. He'd spent the last two nights at the hospital having his operation, and he'd made it very clear he did *not* want me to visit him. As difficult as it had been to stay away, I'd abided by his wishes. I wasn't going to lie, though, I couldn't wait for tomorrow when the hospital was expected to release him.

Barbara chuckled. "Someone sounds as if they're missing someone," she said.

I arched a brow. "Yeah, like I'd miss a toothache."

Liar.

I missed him more than I cared to admit. And so did Bandit. The poor little thing spent his time wandering from room to room, looking for Upton, his big soulful eyes sad and lost. Even letting him sleep on my bed hadn't cheered him up. Only one thing would achieve that—Upton returning home.

Once dogs fell in love, that was it. No escape for the owner. And no substitute for them, either. Bandit tolerated me, but it was Upton he wanted.

"You don't fool me," Barbara stated. "I've got too many years behind me. I see the way you look at him—and I see the way he looks at you, too."

My fingers automatically went to my lips. After Upton kissed me the day before his hospital visit, he'd studiously avoided me. By the time I'd arrived for work the following morning, suitcase in hand, he'd already left, and Barbara had passed on the message that I was to stay here taking care of Bandit and under no circumstances was I to go to see him at the hospital.

"Where is his family, Barbara?" I asked, more willing to ask questions now I knew for certain Upton wouldn't appear on silent feet and castigate me for butting into his private life. "Apart from Sebastian and Antonio, he's had no visitors since I started working here. And we all know he doesn't leave the house unless he absolutely has no other choice."

Barbara's lips thinned. I'd come to recognize that as a sign that something displeased or disappointed her.

"His mama died when he was eleven, God rest her soul." She crossed herself. "His father remarried, and he and his new wife had Jenna. After what happened... well, his stepmother disowned him. She blames him, you see, but nowhere near as much as he blames himself. And, well, his father was caught between two people he loves. He does come by occasionally, but not very often."

My chest tightened. Poor Upton. He'd lost the two most important women in his life, and then his father basically abandoned him at a time he had needed him the most.

The parallels with my own life sucked the breath from my lungs. The only difference was the experience. Zak and my mom could have blamed me for what happened to Zak, but instead, they'd cocooned me in love and care, and Mom, in particular, had pulled us both through a horrendous time.

Not once had either of them uttered a single word of recrimination.

Unlike what Upton had gone through.

"How awful," I murmured. The need for some fresh air came over me, and I got to my feet. "I might take Bandit for a walk."

"All right, dear," Barbara said, shaping the raw dough ready for the oven.

I fetched Bandit's lead and went in search of him. I found him curled up outside Upton's bedroom, waiting for his master to return. He brightened when he saw the lead and jumped up, allowing me to clip it to his collar.

"Come on, boy. Let's get some steps in."

The weather had cooled considerably over the last couple of days, thank goodness. Maybe fall had finally set in. I slipped out the front gates and crossed the road, then ducked down a flight of stone steps partially hidden by an overgrown bush. The steps led to the beach. I'd discovered them a couple of weeks ago when Upton had pissed me off and I'd needed to cool down before I throttled him. In front of him, I maintained a cool persona. To act any other way would hand victory to him, and Hell would freeze over first. But my ability to stay calm under pressure didn't mean I was a robot. I just refused to give Upton the satisfaction of knowing he'd annoyed me. He'd revel in that, and I'd deny him the chance to do so if it was the last thing I did.

Apart from a few surfers riding the white-topped waves, the beach was fairly quiet. I unclipped Bandit's lead, and he took off running. A whistle brought him scurrying back to my side, and I smiled, gave him a treat, then set him on his way again.

I'd wanted to test his recall, and from what I could see, Upton's training sessions were working. Not that he ever walked Bandit outside of the grounds of his house. As soon as he recovered from this operation, I'd make getting Upton to leave his house more often my next goal. He was a young man with decades ahead of him. He couldn't spend his life locked behind the walls of his home, no matter how big or luxurious it was. I'd promised Sebastian I'd do my best to help him, and now that he'd given up trying to force me to quit, it was time to move on to the next phase of his recuperation—whether he wanted to or not.

I stayed out about an hour, but when Bandit lay on the sand and refused to budge, I got the message. Luckily, he was only small and light, and easily fit into the crook of my arm. The second I put him down when we returned to Upton's place, he meandered toward Upton's office—his other favorite hideaway. He liked to sleep beneath the desk, and Upton—despite his 'I don't care about the damn dog' pretense—had purchased another dog bed and placed it there for him so he'd be comfortable.

The kitchen smelled of freshly baked bread, but there was no sign of Barbara. My stomach grumbled, and I made a quick sandwich and took it outside to eat in the shade.

I didn't like being in this house without Upton.

It didn't feel right.

I put my plate in the dishwasher and wandered upstairs. My room was on the same level as Upton's, just a few doors down, but as I passed by his bedroom, I poked my head around the door and then, without permission, my legs took me inside. The memory of the last time I'd entered this room uninvited came flooding back. The sight of Upton's scarred back, the flash of anger in his eyes when he'd caught sight of me, the way he'd thrown the lamp, narrowly missing my head. A normal person might've run at that point, but he and I… we were connected by our joint pain. He had no clue—because I hadn't shared my guilt with him—but I knew. Complete strangers but such similar painful, life-changing experiences.

It helped me connect to him in a way those other 'companions' couldn't have hoped to. It guided me when he was being particularly difficult because I could empathize.

I sat on the edge of his bed, and then I lay down, my head on his pillow, breathing in his masculine scent. Fifteen months ago, my life had ended, but applying for this job had kick-started my heart into beating again.

Into hoping again.

I'd seen flickers of the same hope in Upton, more so over the last couple of weeks. The kiss we'd shared three days ago, one I'd reciprocated this time, had meant something. He might have avoided me for the rest of that day and taken himself off to the hospital before I arrived the following morning, but he didn't fool me.

He'd started off treating me with disdain and antipathy.

Then he'd tried silence.

Followed by anger.

Was the next step acceptance that we were both ready to move on with our lives? To forget the past and embrace the future?

Only time would tell.

~

"Can you drive?" Upton's gruff voice came down the line.

"Yes," I said. "What do you need?"

He paused, then let out a long, resigned sigh. "Apparently the drugs they've given me for the discomfort means I'm not allowed to get behind the wheel for another twenty-four hours.

Can you jump in a cab, come to the hospital, and then drive me home in my car?"

My heart pinched at the despair in his tone. He didn't want to ask for my help, or anyone else's. It had cost him dearly to reach out for support.

Damn frustrating, stubborn male.

"I'm on my way."

The cab driver dropped me off outside the main entrance to the hospital, and I paid him and jumped out. I looked around, searching for Upton. No sign. He must have decided to wait inside, avoiding the midday sun.

I entered through a set of sliding doors, immediately spotting him standing with his shoulder against the wall next to a huge potted plant. He straightened as I approached, but when he took a step, he winced and hissed through his teeth.

"Didn't they give you any painkillers to take home with you?" I asked.

"Yes."

"Have you taken them?"

"No."

"Upton," I chastised.

"Here are the keys," he said, handing them over. "Car's parked in the lot across the street. Fourth row back, about halfway down. It's the SUV we went to the vet's appointment in, so you should recognize it."

I could have started an argument right there, but it was more important to get him home and settled, and then I'd force the damn painkillers down his throat whether he wanted to take them or not.

By the time I arrived in his car, he'd made his way outside. I jumped out and opened the door, but as I tried to help him get in, he growled at me.

"Stop fucking fussing."

"Suit yourself."

Men. Stubborn assholes, the bunch of them. Zak had been the same, wanting to do everything himself, despite the pain it'd caused.

Upton struggled to fasten his seat belt. On his third attempt, he finally shot me an irritated glare. I suppressed a grin, clipped it into place, and put the car in drive. He stared out the window the entire journey home, the only sound an odd hiss whenever the car hit a bump in the road, followed by my mumbled apology, which he didn't respond to.

When we arrived at his house, I stopped the car as close to the entrance as I could get and cut the engine, then ran around to his side to open his door. He climbed out, his face creased in pain.

"Does it hurt very much?" I asked.

"No, Izabelle. It's like being kissed by butterflies," he replied sarcastically.

"Jackass," I muttered, heading inside with him trailing behind.

Bandit must have smelled his owner because he came skidding over the marble floor at a hundred miles an hour, yipping and jumping up at Upton the second he stepped one foot inside the house. Upton tried to bend down to pet him but couldn't quite manage it. I scooped Bandit into my arms and held him up so he could say hello properly. There were those who thought the idea of smiling dogs was fantasyland, but anyone who saw Bandit's face when Upton scratched behind his ear and said a few words couldn't help being converted.

"Can you keep him with you for a while?" Upton asked. "I'm going upstairs to rest."

"Sure," I said.

As Upton walked away, Bandit started barking and struggled to escape from my arms. I had to hold on tight, my throat thick with emotion while Upton painfully, one very slow stair at a time, went upstairs. By now, Barbara had joined me, but when I made a move to try to help him, she stopped me, shaking her head.

"Leave him," she said. "He won't thank you. Trust me on that."

12

Upton

"How are you feeling today?"

Izabelle breezed in carrying a tray. She set it on my nightstand then floated across the thick carpeting of my bedroom to fling open the heavy drapes. I blinked, my retinas protesting at the brilliant sunlight.

"Fuck's sake, are you trying to blind me?" I grabbed a spare pillow and slammed it over my face, sinking me back into darkness.

"I see your mood hasn't improved since yesterday."

Her voice was muffled, but I heard her tone well enough. It reeked of tolerance to my exasperation, which only served to increase my irritation further. The woman had the patience of a fucking saint. No matter how many times I snapped at her, or railed on her as a way to distract myself from the post-operative pain—and the sheer humiliation of her witnessing my incapacitation—she simply smiled and continued bustling about as if I hadn't behaved insufferably.

She whipped the pillow off my face and tossed it to one side. "I've brought you some breakfast. Do you want me to help you sit up?"

Not fucking likely.

"I'm not helpless, Izabelle."

I proved that statement completely false when I struggled to shift myself upright without searing pain in my back making me hiss loudly. She made a move to help. I shot her a glare and held up a finger.

"Do not touch me. I can manage."

She let out a soft sigh but left me to labor on alone while she poured strong-smelling coffee into a cup. I eventually got myself into a semi-upright position, but the effort left me panting as if I'd run up a hill at full tilt. I waited for her to make a comment, and I had a sharp retort ready, but one thing I'd begun to learn about Izabelle was that she often did the opposite of what I expected.

I sank back against the pillows and took the cup of coffee from her outstretched hand. "Thanks," I muttered, sounding anything but grateful.

"I brought your painkillers, too."

She held out her palm, two white pills nestling there.

"I'm not taking them."

"Yes, you are."

"I don't like the way they make me feel."

She arched an eyebrow. "You mean pain free? You'd rather suffer?"

I made a frustrated noise and snatched the damn pills from her hand, washing them down with a mouthful of coffee. "Happy?" I snapped.

"Delighted."

She shot me a grin. I responded with a growl.

I ate the omelet she'd brought while she sat on the edge of my bed and rabbited on about something and nothing in that uncanny way she had to fill uncomfortable silences. I thought about telling her to shut the fuck up but swallowed the words instead. She didn't deserve my wrath, no matter how patiently she put up with my snappy attitude. Sure, I was in pain from the operation, and I despised her seeing me in such a vulnerable state, but that didn't excuse me treating her horribly.

My father once said to me—at a time when he'd bothered to acknowledge I existed—that my prideful attitude was my kryptonite, and I didn't disagree. But Izabelle wasn't the hired help. Not any longer. The kiss we'd shared the day before I went into the hospital had shifted the ground on which we stood, changing the dynamics of our relationship. Once I'd fully recovered, I'd make it up to her, somehow.

I handed her my empty plate, and she set it down on the tray, then got to her feet.

"Do you need help getting to the bathroom?" she asked and then, with a quirk to her lips, added, "or maybe I should just bring you a bedpan."

The growl deep in my chest reminded me of a grizzly bear, but instead of heeding the warning and shifting into retreat, she grinned even wider.

"I'll take that as a no." She picked up the tray. "Call me if you need anything."

"Don't hold your breath," I groused at her retreating back.

I waited until she'd closed the door then gingerly folded back the covers. This wouldn't be easy, but I'd crawl into the bathroom before I'd accept help from Izabelle. Call me a stubborn ass—it was the truth—but there were occasions when holding on to my pride was far more important than any pain my arrogance caused.

And this was one of them.

Something's different.

I lay in bed with my eyes closed, trying to figure out what it was.

And then I did.

My back no longer hurt. Three days of painful spasms and finally, I felt almost normal. Exactly as my surgeon promised. I really must send that man a good bottle of single malt.

I climbed out of bed and practiced a stretch. A twinge, but nothing I couldn't handle. I peeled off the square of gauze over my wound and checked it out in the mirror. Yeah, that looked much better. I scanned the aftercare sheet my surgeon had passed along. Good. I didn't have to wear a covering any longer.

Flicking on the shower, I quickly washed, dabbed the skin around the dissolvable stitches, and then dressed in a loose T-shirt and jeans. I expected to find Bandit curled up outside my bedroom door, like Izabelle informed me he had every morning, but he wasn't there. I padded downstairs, gaining more evidence I was well on the mend when nothing hurt, and entered the kitchen, my pulse jolting in anticipation of seeing Izabelle while standing on my own two feet and not in the prostrate position of the last few days.

She wasn't there, and nor was Bandit. I poked my head outside. Nope, not out by the pool either. Damn. Where was she?

And why was I standing here with disappointment lowering my shoulders?

Somehow over the last few months, Izabelle had wormed her way inside the steel cage I'd built around myself since Jenna's death and my father's capitulation to Jenice's demands that he cut me off at the knees.

I thought back to when I'd woken up in the hospital after the bomb exploded and learned that we'd lost Jenna and his platitudes of giving Jenice time, that she'd come around in the end, that he loved me. Words. Pointless words that he hadn't followed up with actions. Jenice hadn't forgiven me, and would never forgive me, and he'd chosen her over his own flesh and blood, his last remaining child.

I didn't blame Jenice. She had every right to hate me—hell, she couldn't hate me more than I did myself—but it hurt like a motherfucker that my father found it so easy to cut me out of his life. I hadn't seen him in more than six months, and I didn't expect that to change any time soon.

I flicked on the coffee machine and poured cream into a cup while I waited for it to brew. The sound of the front door closing reached me, and I craned my neck, a smile edging across my face as Izabelle came toward me with an over-excited Bandit straining on his lead, anxious to reach me.

"Hey, you're up."

I crouched and scooped him into my arms, scratched behind his ears, then set him back on the floor.

"Yeah. Finally, I can look down on you."

She chuckled. "Glad to see you've found your sense of humor at last."

"Who said I'm joking?"

"Jerk," she said, edging me out of the way and making us both a coffee.

"I wondered where you were," I said, my voice low and husky. "When I came downstairs and you weren't here, I thought I'd finally succeeded in chasing you away, especially given how awful I've behaved the last few days."

She stopped what she was doing and turned to face me. "You should know by now that you can't get rid of me that easily."

Reaching out, I clutched a lock of her hair and twisted it around my fingers. "Good."

She swallowed, and her tongue slid along her bottom lip. "Are you still in pain?"

"No." I gave her a wry smile. "Maybe a little."

"Is there anything I can do to help?" she asked, her voice hoarse.

"Yeah." I bent my head. "There is."

I captured her mouth, my tongue easing her lips apart. She smelled of peaches and lemons, and I breathed her in, gathering her in my arms. I expected her to push me away, to somehow want to punish me for my appalling treatment of her ever since I'd been released from the hospital.

Except she didn't push me away.

Instead, her arms came up around my neck, and she knitted her fingers into my hair and plastered herself against my body. Her tits flattened on contact, but her nipples hardened, delicious points made for my mouth.

I burrowed underneath her T-shirt and closed my hand over her breast, encased in a lace bra I wanted to rip off of her. I refrained. We weren't there yet. But damn, she felt so good. Soft and warm and fucking perfect.

When I brushed the pad of my thumb over her nipple, she groaned and arched her back, pressing closer.

Footsteps approached, and we broke apart right before Barbara bustled into the kitchen, her arms full of groceries. We must have both looked guilty because she switched her gaze from Izabelle to me and then back to Izabelle. She set bags full of groceries on top of the kitchen table, a smile tugging at the corners of her mouth.

"Ten bedrooms, twelve bathrooms, four reception rooms, a large pool house, a library, and a backyard filled with hideyholes, and you two kids decide to make out in my domain." She tutted and shook her head. "Dear oh dear."

Heat flooded Izabelle's face, and she ducked her head.

I narrowed my eyes at Barbara. "Hardly kids, and this is my house, so technically you're in *my* domain."

Barbara nudged me out of the way and plucked a pineapple from one of the bags. "I'll concede the first point, but not the second. Now both of you scoot. Out of my kitchen. I have a lot to do today."

"Like what?" I asked, arching an eyebrow. "You're hardly cooking for ten."

"Never you mind," Barbara said, but her eyes when she looked at me were filled with hope. "You're not too old to put over my knee, Upton Barrick."

I chuckled. "Fine."

Izabelle gratefully took the hand I offered, and we left Barbara to whatever she had planned. As soon as we were out of earshot, I whispered in Izabelle's ear, "Anytime you want me to put you over my knee, just say the word."

Izabelle chuckled. "Gettin' ahead of yourself there, Mr. Billionaire." And then she groaned. "How embarrassing."

"If you think that's embarrassing, you've led a sheltered life."

She peered up at me. "I bet you got up to all sorts of mischief in the past."

I grinned down at her. "You have no idea."

She didn't return my smile, though. Instead, her expression grew thoughtful.

"You've changed."

I canted my head. "Changed how?" I asked, except I knew. And she was right. Not only did I appear different to her, but I *felt* different. Freer. Optimistic about the future. I had a long way to go. I still hated going out in public, and my moods wildly swung from one extreme to another, and guilt was a concrete slab around my neck. But there was no doubt about it. I'd changed from the man I'd been a few short months ago before Izabelle came into my life. And the addition of Bandit—as much as I'd berated her for introducing him into my life—had given me something to think about other than wallowing in the pit of despair I'd occupied since that horrific night.

"Are you busy this morning?"

She'd ignored my question for one reason only; she must have seen in my face that I already knew the answer.

"Yeah," I said. "I'm maxed. You've seen how crazy my schedule is."

She narrowed her eyes. "Y'know, I think I preferred the Upton that either snapped at me or ignored me completely."

I slung an arm around her shoulders in a proprietary fashion, and it felt right. Like my arm belonged there, holding her close to me. "You and I both know that's a lie."

"Sarcasm is the lowest form of wit," she said.

Clasping a hand over my heart, I said, "You wound me, Miss Laker."

She shook her head. "You're such a jerk."

I laughed. "Tell me, what did you have in mind?"

"I have to go pick up something for my brother, and it'd be easier if you drove me as long as you're feeling up to it. You don't have to get out of the car," she added hurriedly. "But it'd help me out a lot."

I pressed a kiss to her temple. "Anything for you."

13

BELLE

Anything for you.

He'd kissed me, put an arm around my shoulder, joked about giving me a spanking, and then uttered those words. *What's going on here?*

"Are you sure the doctors only operated on your back?" I asked with an impish grin. "Maybe they injected you with a few 'be nice to Belle' genes, too."

He poked his tongue into his cheek and raked his gaze over me. "Y'know, if you're ready for me to put you over my knee, it's easier and faster to just ask."

I slid from underneath his arm and skipped out of the way. "Down, boy."

Snagging me around the waist, he pulled me flush against his body and circled his hips. "Too late for that."

His lips captured mine again, and my stomach clenched and rolled in that delicious way a man's expert touch produced.

Oh, who am I kidding?

I'd loved Marin. He'd been my first, and I'd been his, which meant neither of us were hugely experienced. The way Upton splayed his large hands across my back, how his tongue stroked mine, the feel of his soft yet firm lips, well, it was different. More intense. He made me feel… needy. Wet. Desperate for more.

And guilty.

What are you doing?

I drew back. "I'm sorry," I said, my eyes cast on the floor. "It's just…"

He clipped me under the chin, lifting my head. "Too much too soon?"

I nibbled on my lower lip. "Maybe a little."

He nodded. "I can wait. We all have a history, and one day soon, you'll tell me yours."

"Cocky much?" I asked, relief swarming through me. He could have taken my rejection badly, but instead, his kindness and understanding of a situation he had no idea about made me want to kiss him again. Perhaps that was his plan? Force me to go to him, to beg for his touch.

I could see how that might happen. But not yet. I needed time alone to get my head around the shift in our relationship.

"Come on," he said. "You can pick which car we take."

"Better make it the SUV," I said. "It's a pretty big package."

The arch to his brow and the way he lowered his eyes to his groin had me laughing out loud. "Men," I said, raising my eyes upward. "You're all the same."

"True," he said. "Except I can back up my claims."

I suppressed a tremor of pleasure. The idea of Upton parting my thighs, settling between my legs, and pushing his huge—

"You're blushing." His laughter interrupted my dirty thoughts. "And I know exactly why."

I ground my teeth. "There's such a thing as overconfident. Bring back reclusive, silent Upton. I liked him better."

"Sure you did," he said.

I growled, and he laughed.

"Never play poker, Izabelle. You suck at hiding your thoughts."

"Whatever," I mumbled childishly.

He laughed harder and opened the garage, grabbing the keys to the SUV. "Right," he said, snapping his seat belt into place. "Where are we going?"

I gave him the zip code, and he punched it into the fancy satnav system, then drove onto the road. My eyes were drawn to his strong hands on the wheel as he negotiated the winding roads with ease. I loved his hands. Not that I'd ever tell him that. His confidence was making a speedy comeback, so the very last thing he needed was further encouragement. My head spun at his change in attitude. Then again, he'd been in a fair bit of discomfort since his operation. I didn't blame him for being moody.

The closer we got to the store where I'd ordered Zak's wheelchair, the more excited I became. This would make such a difference to Zak's life and give him more independence. And I could make this happen because of this job. In another two months, I'd be able to afford a little car. I'd already been looking at a few around ten years old that were in my price bracket. That would do me just fine. And then I'd be able to take Zak out. With transportation and a motorized wheelchair, we could visit lots of places he hadn't been able to go since the accident.

Upton frowned as he nosed the car into the parking lot and stopped. He shifted in his seat to face me. "Is this the right place?"

"Yep. This is it. Want to come inside, or would you rather wait here?"

"Why do you need a wheelchair?"

"It's not for me. It's for my brother."

I pressed down on the handle and climbed out. Upton surprised me by following suit.

"Your brother is in a wheelchair?"

I nodded.

"I'm sorry."

Sorrow clutched my chest, and I took a deep breath through my nose to quell the guilt rising inside. "Me, too."

"Was he born paralyzed?"

I shook my head. "No. He had an accident."

"What happened?" he asked gently.

"Not now." I swallowed. "Today is a happy day. With the money I've earned from this job, I can afford to buy him a motorized wheelchair. He's so excited. It'll afford him so much more independence."

I set off toward the entrance, half expecting Upton to return to the car and wait for me there. Instead, he caught up to me and threaded his fingers through mine. I squeezed and looked up at him. "Thanks for helping me. I'd originally planned to pick it up and take it on the bus until I realized the weight of the damn thing. And delivery was hellishly expensive."

"Anything for you," he repeated, and my stomach twisted.

We walked inside, the bell over the door dinging to signal our arrival.

"Be right with you," a voice called from out back, and seconds later, the man I'd dealt with when I'd ordered the chair a couple of weeks earlier appeared. He glanced at Upton, stared at his scar for a snap too long, then swiftly turned to me. "Ah, Miss Laker, correct?"

I gnashed my teeth together. No wonder Upton hated going out in public if that was the reaction he got. It amazed me how people treated those who were a little different from the general population. Zak suffered it all the time. Stares, unwarranted help, people thinking he was incapable of doing anything on his own, and not even bothering to ask before opening doors or pushing him without his permission. Some people pissed me off.

"That's right. I got your email," I said, my tone on the curt side. "Today is the first day I've had a chance to come by."

His face bloomed with color. Good. He got the message.

"Not a problem at all, Miss Laker. Is your car parked out front?"

"It is."

"Great. I'll bring it out to you."

We returned to Upton's car. I opened my mouth to apologize—not that it was my apology to make—but the store owner appeared from the rear of the building with a huge cardboard box before I could. Between the three of us, we loaded it into the trunk of Upton's car with me constantly fussing about his back, and him glowering in response. I signed the paperwork and climbed in to Upton's car without even saying goodbye. Maybe that would make the store owner think twice next time. I mean, he sold wheelchairs for a living. Dealing with disabilities should be the norm for him.

"What a jerk," I said as I reached for my seat belt.

A tic materialized in his jaw, and he kept his gaze dead ahead. "I'm used to it."

"Doesn't make it right."

"Forget it." He started the engine. "Where to next?"

"Well," I said, grinning. "Buckle up. You're about to meet my family."

I swore he turned a little green.

Upton managed to park right outside our house—thank goodness. I didn't fancy lugging that box too far. I darted inside to fetch Mom, but by the time I returned with her, Upton already had the box out of the car and sitting on the sidewalk. I shot him a glare. He shrugged in response.

"Mom, this is my boss, Upton." I smirked at my introduction.

"Lovely to meet you, Mrs. Laker," Upton said, shaking my mom's hand.

Mom—God bless her—paid zero attention to his scar. Instead, she hit him with a beaming smile and said, "My, my. No wonder my daughter didn't hesitate to move in to take care of you. I'll happily take on another job if there's an opening."

My mouth dropped open. "Mom!" I admonished.

Upton burst out laughing. "To be fair, Mrs. Laker, I have a feeling you might not be quite as bossy as your daughter, so we should discuss the matter further."

"Hey." I gave him a sharp dig with my elbow which earned me a wink and an even wider smile.

Mom's eyes narrowed, and I suppressed a groan. Dammit. She knew me far too well. No doubt tonight's dinner conversation would center on Upton and me, and what the heck was going on.

Answer: I wish I knew.

"Here," Mom said, bending her knees to grab one side of the box. "Let's get this inside. Zak is beside himself with excitement. Belle, you carry this end with me, and Upton, if you can take the other end, that'd be great."

We maneuvered the awkward box into the house without too much trouble. Leaving it in the entranceway, I walked into the kitchen with Mom and Upton trailing behind, chatting as if they'd known each other for ages.

Zak appeared from the living room, his eyes lighting up. "Hey, sis. Is it here?"

I kicked my head back. "Yep. We left it out there. This is Upton, by the way. Mom's new boss."

Upton snorted with laughter while Zak merely looked confused. "Huh?"

I shook my head. "Never mind."

Upton came over and greeted Zak. "Good to meet you. Do you want a hand unpacking it?"

Zak nodded. "That'd be great." He wheeled himself out of the kitchen toward the front of the house. Upton followed. Not once did he grab Zak's chair to push him. I could have kissed him.

"Well, well." Mom craned her neck and peered down the hallway. "He's a sight for sore eyes, isn't he?"

I poked my tongue into my cheek and lifted my right shoulder. "Can't say I've noticed."

Mom raised both eyebrows. "If that's true, then we need to make an appointment with the eye doctor."

I huffed and stomped off to join Upton and Zak, Mom's chuckling following me out of the kitchen. Having a mother who knew you as well as mine knew me was both a blessing and a curse. I'd managed to keep her inquisitiveness at bay by only telling her stories about how difficult he was, but now that she'd seen us together, she'd homed in and seen right through the shallow veneer I'd erected.

Within fifteen minutes, we had Zak's wheelchair unpacked. He hoisted himself into it, and soon after, he was tearing around the house as if he'd had it for days.

"I owe you, sis," Zak said. "This will make getting around much easier. And when you've saved up for that car, maybe we could take a trip. I'll be able to go much further in this baby."

I drowned in Zak's happiness. That I'd been able to do this small thing to enhance his independence meant the world to me. Those first few weeks when Upton's attitude had challenged every strand of my patience faded into insignificance. *This*, Zak's delight, made every single second worth it.

His generosity of spirit still humbled me, even after all this time. I liked to think that if the situation was reversed, I'd have been the same, except I couldn't say hand on heart that I would.

"You and I both know who owes who around here." I squeezed his shoulder. "But yeah, a trip sounds terrific."

We stayed for a coffee, but when Upton winced as he stood to put his cup in the sink, I suggested we make a move. He'd done far more than he should have, lugging a heavy wheelchair around. I'd have tried to stop him if I'd thought for one minute he'd have listened to a word I said.

Upton drove away, and I waved to Mom and Zak until they disappeared from sight. I flopped back in the soft leather of Upton's car and sighed. "Thanks for helping me. I don't know what I'd have done if you'd refused, other than to pay a small fortune for delivery."

"It's fine," Upton said. "God, you're a fusser."

I folded my arms. "Am not."

"Yes, you are."

I couldn't deny it. Caring for people was in my blood. My earliest memories were of dressing up in a nurse's outfit that Mom bought me one Christmas and forcing Zak to play the patient while I mopped his brow and pretended to listen to his heart through a toy stethoscope. Little did I know back then that I'd end up having to care for him for real.

"What are you thinking about?" Upton asked, jerking me from both happy and sad memories.

"Zak," I said. "A childhood memory of when I'd pretend he was my patient, and I was the nurse taking care of him, much to his chagrin. But he'd always play along, for me." I sighed and nibbled my lip, then shifted my gaze out the window. "We're twins, you know."

"You are?"

"Yeah."

Upton turned down the radio. "What happened?"

I shook my head, my gaze remaining averted. I wasn't ready

to tell him that I was supposed to go to the concert that night, but that I got waylaid and Zak went in my place, hence my crippling guilt at his paralysis. Upton and I were just getting somewhere, and I didn't want to detract from the progress we'd made by turning the focus on me. If I shared what had happened to Zak, then I'd have to tell him about Marin, too, and then he'd know how much we had in common. I wasn't ready to share the similarity of our heartbreaking stories. I wanted him to come around on his own, to want me for me, not because of our common grief.

"I'll stay tonight in case you need anything after today's exertions. But tomorrow, I'm moving back home."

14

Upton

Despite the occasional gentle nudge from me, Izabelle refused to disclose anything further about Zak. My radar was firing, like off the charts. Every time I broached the subject, she'd get this look on her face, and it was an expression I recognized. I saw it often when I stared into the mirror.

Guilt.

Whatever the cause of Zak's disability, Izabelle felt culpable in some way. I couldn't force her to open up to me, but damn, I wanted to try. I wouldn't, though. She'd only clam up, and I'd take that as reason to drill harder, and we'd end up getting nowhere other than thoroughly pissed off at each other. I had no option other than to wait for her to come around and tell me in her own time.

Then again, I hadn't exactly allowed myself to open up either. Izabelle only knew what Sebastian and Garen told her, but nothing directly from me. Maybe if I shared a little of my own pain, she'd feel more comfortable sharing hers. Had to be worth a try.

With my mind made up, I sought her out, eventually tracking her to the library. Her legs were tucked beneath her, and she had her head buried in a book. She glanced up as I entered and smiled, then set down the book.

"Busted."

I flopped down beside her. "Slacking on the job is a sackable offense."

"You won't fire me."

I twirled a lock of her hair around my forefinger. "Oh yeah?"

"Yeah. You like having me around too much. Not that someone as macho as you would ever admit it, but I know the truth."

I chuckled. "How's Zak getting along with the wheelchair?"

She beamed, her evident happiness at what she'd been able to do for her brother only increasing my curiosity even further.

"Terrific. It's given him a lot more independence. He and his best friend, Chad, went to a Lakers game the other day, and just being able to move around more easily means so much to him. He hates relying on others for his care." Her eyes gleamed mischievously. "Sound familiar?"

Her comment about the Lakers had given me an opening, and I took it.

"My dad used to take me to the Lakers games when I was younger."

She sat up straight, her eyes laser focused on mine, all hint of teasing leaving her. "You never mention your dad," she stated, her tone gentle and coaxing.

I shrugged. "What's the point. He prefers to pretend I don't exist."

Her hand rested on my arm, the warmth melting the icy

chill that always descended when I thought about my family. I might have engineered this conversation, but that didn't mean this shit was any easier to talk about.

"Do you want to tell me about it?"

I heaved a sigh and swept a hand over my face. "My dad and I used to be close, especially after my mother died when I was still young. Dad remarried, and he and my stepmother, Jenice, had Jenna soon after. But when she died, all that ended. Jenice blames me, and I blame me. Dad got caught in the middle and chose a side." I snorted a laugh, but there was no mirth in it, only bitterness. "You can guess which side he chose."

Her grip tightened, as did the skin around her mouth as she flattened her lips. "It wasn't your fault."

I didn't respond because I saw no point in arguing. I was to blame. If I'd never taken Jenna and her friend to that concert, she'd still be alive. The terrorist might be the real culprit, but that didn't stop me feeling the way I did.

"You must miss your dad."

I shrugged, sorry I'd started this conversation now, especially as Izabelle showed no signs of sharing her story, which had been the whole reason for picking at this painful scab. I got to my feet. "I could do with some fresh air. Want to take a walk with me?"

She took the hint that the sharing and caring shit was over and glided to her feet. "Sounds good."

~

A couple of days later, I entered the kitchen and found her and Barbara stuffing sandwiches and snacks into a backpack.

"What's going on?"

Izabelle hit me with a blinding smile. "We're getting the heck out of this house and going on a hike. Don't even bother arguing with me. It's a gorgeous day, much cooler than the last few days, and I, for one, am not sitting around here watching the grass grow. Besides, Bandit needs to burn off some steam. I caught him yesterday digging like crazy on the living room rug. I managed to stop him before he destroyed it, but now that he's growing, he needs much more exercise."

I waited until she'd finished. "Sales pitch over?" I asked, arching an eyebrow. "Can I speak now?"

Barbara sniggered. Izabelle crossed her arms over her chest.

"Yes, but if you're—"

"Ah, ah." I waggled my finger. "You've used up your word allowance."

She growled, and my dick twitched. Damn, I wanted her, but I was conscious that we'd done little more than kiss, and she'd given me no come-on signals that she wanted to take things further. Until she did, I'd have to keep jerking off in the shower with the image of her firmly fixed in my mind to satisfy my growing urges.

"A hike sounds like a great idea," I said.

She broke into a broad smile. "Really? I expected you to be an asshole about the idea."

"Charming." I bent down to scoop up Bandit who'd wandered in from God only knew where, wearing a guilty expression. I groaned, fully expecting to find another pair of expensive Italian loafers completely destroyed. Before I'd owned a dog, I wouldn't have believed they had the capability to show guilt, but they absolutely did. His eyes turned soulful, and he often hung his head as if to say "Sorry, but I couldn't help it".

"What have you been up to, you little monster?" I pointlessly asked. If only dogs could talk...

"I'll just finish off here," Izabelle said. "And then we can go."

Ten minutes later, we had the car loaded with food and water, a container for Bandit to drink from, and a few treats in case he wandered off and I needed to coax him to return.

Izabelle had picked one of the quieter trails that were away from the main tourist spots. It took us around forty-five minutes to drive there, and as we pulled into the parking lot, Bandit must have sensed the approaching exciting activity and he barked and tugged on his harness. I shrugged into the backpack, and we both coated any exposed skin liberally in sunscreen. Bandit took no notice of the water I poured for him, far too interested in the newness of his latest adventure. I unhooked his lead, and he took off running. I didn't let him get too far before I called him back. He returned immediately and plunked on his rump, his tongue lolling out the side of his mouth. Once he'd snaffled the treat, he sped away, but stopped every few seconds to turn around and make sure we were still there.

"You've done a great job training him," Izabelle said.

I clasped her hand and rubbed my thumb over her knuckles. "Your training of me hasn't gone so badly either."

She laughed. "It was only a matter of time."

I lifted her hand to my lips and pressed a kiss to the back of it. "Thank you. For putting up with me. For sticking around and refusing to give up. For encouraging me to get out more. For suggesting this as a trip out, rather than something more... populated."

"I knew you wouldn't want to go to a crowded beach or a theme park, or anything like that." She pushed her sunglasses on top of her head and squinted up at me. "I get it, Upton. Really, I do."

I nodded. "I believe you."

We fell into silence, partly because of the energy needed to hike the steep mountain. I worked out regularly enough—in my gym—but hill walking took a different kind of fitness, and the compression on my chest and the way my lungs burned told me I needed to do this a little more often. I shifted my gaze to Izabelle. Maybe, with her by my side, I would.

We hardly passed anyone on our way to the summit, and when we reached the top, only two other couples had also summited, both a fair distance away. I dropped the backpack and gave Bandit a drink. Unfolding the picnic blanket proved tricky when he kept trying to lie on it before I was done rolling it out. In the end, Izabelle picked him up to allow me to finish the task. The second I had, he leaped from Izabelle's arms and plunked himself right in the middle as if to say "Mine".

I nudged him out of the way. "This dog is taking liberties," I grumbled.

"Well, you know what they say. There's no such thing as a bad dog, only a bad owner."

I gathered her in my arms and pulled her flush against me. "Is that so?" I murmured. "Then maybe I'll have to show you just how bad I can be."

I kissed her, starting off slow and exploratory, but as I'd learned was the case when my lips connected with Izabelle's, passion exploded between us. I rubbed my cock on her clit, and she moaned into my mouth. Fuck if that didn't give me an erection as hard as an iron bar.

Just as I was getting into my stride, the damned dog got jealous and scratched at my leg. I tried to shake him off but failed miserably.

I broke off the kiss. "That's it," I said. "The dog has to go."

She laughed and sat on the blanket, tugging me down next to her. "I know you don't mean that."

"If he fucks up the next kiss, you're damn right I mean it."

She cradled my face, right over my scar. I flinched.

"No one sees your scars, Upton."

I shook my head. "Bullshit. People stare at me all the time. At the hospital, on the street. Sitting at a set of traffic lights minding my own goddamn business."

On that occasion, the young guy who'd yelled "Fucking freak" through his window while trying to impress his deadbeat friends, who all thought it highly amusing to yell slurs at a complete stranger, had lived to regret his words. I'd gotten out of my car, stormed around to the drivers' side, yanked open his door, and slammed my fist into his face. Blood had splattered the windshield, his nose busted from a single punch.

Served the fucker right.

But I couldn't fight the world. And so I'd withdrawn from public life, only going out when I absolutely had to.

Until her.

Izabelle.

Somehow, the walls I'd built lay crumbled around my feet, and it was all thanks to the woman sitting beside me.

"I don't mean *people*, Upton," she said. "Who gives a shit about them? I mean those who matter. Sebastian, Antonio, Barbara, Paolo. Your other friends from your company." She nibbled on her lip, and her gaze rested on my face. "Me. I only see you."

My stomach flipped over, and I spun her on her back. I kissed her and burrowed underneath her jacket and T-shirt, seeking out her soft, round breasts. Her nipple pebbled beneath my thumb, and I pinched it.

She tore her lips away from mine, her eyes seeking me out. "We're in public," she panted.

"Do you want me to stop?"

"Yes, I mean, no."

I tugged down the cup of her bra and sucked the point into my mouth, tasting her. Sweet. Delectable. Heaven.

Mine.

"What if someone sees," she said, her skin reddening beautifully.

"Then let's put on a show."

Even Bandit must have caught the mood, staying as he did on the corner of the blanket and looking toward the other hikers almost as if he was keeping watch.

Good dog.

I released her other breast and pushed them together, then sucked on both nipples at once. She went crazy, grinding against me, her hips seeking more friction, more attention. Just more. I rubbed her through the thick denim, but it wasn't enough. With a single flick, the button on her jeans came undone. Her zipper was next, and then I pushed two fingers inside her, right where she needed me to be. Right where *I* needed to be.

"You feel like a goddamn dream," I muttered. "Like the best dream I've ever had."

She mumbled something, but she was so far gone by this time, lost in a haze of desire, the words made no sense. I flicked her clit then pressed down with the pad of my thumb, moving my fingers in and out of her, curving inside to scrape the front wall of her pussy.

Her muscles clenched, gripping me hard. Fuck, I needed her to do that around my cock. *She's close.*

"Upton, God, please."

I bit her nipple and simultaneously scraped my thumbnail over her clit. It wasn't gentle. She didn't want or need gentle. She crested and cried out. I swallowed her screams, pushing my tongue into her mouth, wishing it was her pussy. We needed somewhere more private before I could taste her there. My bedroom as soon as we got home, perhaps.

"Jesus. God. I've never... God, I've never done anything like that in public."

Her face pinked up again. It suited her. I grinned, unashamed.

"Then you've led a very sheltered life."

"Says the hermit," she retorted, shoving her tits back inside her bra.

"Spoil my view why don't you," I said, my eyes locked on her chest as she tugged her T-shirt back into place.

She shot a glance at the other couples, relief flooding her face when she realized they weren't paying us any attention, too busy checking out the amazing view from up here.

"Relax." I lay on my side and propped my head up on my elbow, drawing figures of eight on her smooth, flat belly. "How long has it been since you've had an orgasm?"

The color returned to her cheeks. "I'm not telling you that?"

"Why not?"

She averted her gaze. "Because."

"Very adult response," I drawled. "Come on, Belle. I want to know."

Her forehead creased. "You just called me Belle."

I wrinkled my nose. "I guess now I've had my fingers inside you, I should call you by the name you prefer. Now stop stalling. How long."

"Fine. Thirty seconds."

I chuckled. *Clever girl.*

"And the time before that."

"I don't like the turn of this conversation," she grumbled.

"Okay, I'll go first. The last time I came inside a woman was five days before the bomb that killed my sister."

Her eyes widened, and she winced a little at my blunt statement. "The last time you had an orgasm was more than fifteen months ago."

I shook my head. "That's not what I said. Believe me, I've had plenty of orgasms. We need them. It's nothing to be ashamed of. I had an incredible one watching you climb out of my pool. Yellow bikini. Sooooo hot."

Her jaw clanged open. "You watched me?" she whispered.

"Oh yeah." I flicked my tongue over my lips. "Best orgasm I've had in a while. Damn near blew my head off."

"I-I... You're unbelievable."

I gave her a crooked smile. "I can't deny it. It's true. I am."

She tutted. "I'm berating you, not congratulating you."

I grinned, snagged her around the waist, and kissed her. "It's all the same to me, angel." I ran my nose down hers. "Your turn."

Her eyes took on a faraway look, and then they filled with tears. "The night before my fiancé died."

15

Belle

What the hell have you done?

Upton stared at me, surprise, curiosity, and, yes, a hint of jealousy etched across his face. "You were engaged?"

Goddammit, Belle.

"Yes. My high school sweetheart."

He shifted his position, putting a little distance between us. Whether that was for me or for him, I didn't know.

"How did he die?"

I shook my head, still not ready to have this conversation despite what we'd just done, how close we'd grown over the last few weeks. The longer my subterfuge went on, the harder it became to tell him. "Do you mind if I don't talk about it?"

He nodded, twisting a lock of my hair around his forefinger. "I understand." He smiled wryly. "Boy, do I ever. Y'know, after Jenna died, it was months before I could take a full breath. Even now, there are times when I feel like I'm drowning. But these last few weeks, it's gotten easier. I don't think I'll ever fully shed the pain of losing my sister, but you, Belle, you open my eyes to the possibility of a normal life."

His words, spoken with such honesty and feeling, were so close to my own that I struggled not to spill my guts, right then and there, but despite his increasing frankness, something I couldn't explain still held me back.

I drew my teeth over my bottom lip. "I'm so sorry about your sister."

He lowered his head and briefly kissed me. "I'm sorry about your fiancé."

I smiled, desperate to bring a little light to the grief-stricken direction our conversation had taken. "We're a pair, aren't we?"

A chuckle fell from his lips, and he sat up and then held out his hand to me. "Shall we eat? I'm starved."

Upton gave Bandit a dog chew to keep him occupied, and we dug into our picnic. An hour later, with the backpack significantly lighter, we made our way back down the mountainside. As soon as Upton put Bandit into his harness, he lay down on the car seat and promptly fell asleep.

"Dogs are so lucky," I said, righting an ear that had turned inside out. "I could do with a nap myself."

Upton tapped his watch. "You're on the clock until five."

I rolled my eyes. "Slave driver."

His gaze rested on my face and then slipped to my chest. "You can take a nap in my bed."

My throat tightened, and I forced a swallow past a lump in my throat. Was I ready for that yet? I'd only ever slept with Marin, and we'd dated for almost a year before we took that final step. I mean, we did lots of other stuff before then, but... Then again, I wasn't a teenager any longer. I was a woman, and here standing before me was a man, a beautiful, damaged, reclusive man with many obstacles of his own still to overcome.

The problem was that he'd enchanted me, but I also feared the feelings he stimulated. I was terrified of taking such a huge leap and risk getting hurt. Upton had cut himself off from normal life, and in my head, that made me a rebound of sorts, someone he could practice on, test the waters with, and then once he was ready, forge out into the world he'd left behind.

And leave me along with it.

"I-I can't. I'm sorry. It's too soon."

"Because you're still in love with your fiancé?" he asked, not unkindly.

"No, it's not that. It's..." I couldn't explain, not without basically telling him I didn't trust him.

"You think I'm using you."

"No. Yes. Maybe." I covered my face with my hands and rubbed. "That came out all wrong."

He captured my wrists and tugged, forcing me to face him. "You don't have to explain. I can see why you might think you're some kind of therapy for me. Only time will show you that isn't true. Even before Jenna died, I wasn't what you'd call a player." He chuckled. "At least not as much as some of my friends. I dated women, sure, but I didn't jump from one bed to another." He dropped a kiss on my forehead. "Shall we head off?"

Silence enveloped us as Upton drove back to his place, and when I couldn't stand it any longer, I asked the question that had burned me since he'd mentioned it. "The woman you slept with before your sister passed away. What happened to her?"

His lips twisted to one side. "She ended it before I'd even left the hospital. We hadn't dated for long. A couple of months maybe, but she couldn't even bear to look at me. At this." He pointed to the jagged scar that, for me, only added to his allure.

"Then you're well rid of her," I said, folding my arms across my chest defensively.

He chuckled, and he grazed his knuckles down my cheek. "I kinda like you sticking up for me."

"Some people suck."

"Yes," he said, nodding. "They do."

The atmosphere lifted, although we shared no more than a few words for the rest of the journey. Upton eased the car into the garage, cut the engine, then shifted in his seat to face me.

"Two things," he said. "Firstly, I don't want you catching the bus any longer, not when I have all these cars sitting here gathering dust. So, take your pick."

My jaw dropped. "You're giving me a car?"

"*Loaning* you a car," he qualified. "As long as you work for me, it's yours. Call it a company perk."

Seizing the opportunity to tease him, I said, "I think you'll find I work for Sebastian and Garen. Their names are on the contract I signed."

He growled. "You work for me."

I laughed, relieved the awkward atmosphere had dissolved. "Gotcha."

He moved fast, a blur, and his mouth took mine in a kiss that sent shivers to the top of my head and the tips of my toes. When he came up for air, I couldn't catch my breath.

"You work for me," he reiterated. "I don't give a shit which ROGUES director signed the contract."

"Yes, boss," I said, rather enjoying his proprietary attitude. "Whatever you say."

He groaned. "Jesus, when I finally get you into bed, please repeat that."

"Sure of yourself, aren't you?"

His eyes glazed over, only for a moment. "I used to be," he murmured.

I cradled his face and pressed my lips to his. "Give me some time."

"Take as much as you need."

"Now," I said. "About this car. I can't take it. In a couple months I'll have enough saved to buy a car of my own, and I'd rather not be indebted."

"In case I use it to lure you to bed." He winked. "Seriously, take it. If you want to give it back when you buy your own, that's fine, but until then, please humor me. We're coming into wintertime soon when the nights will get dark earlier. I'd rather you weren't standing on the street waiting for public transport at that time."

"Okay," I said reluctantly. "But only until I've saved up enough money."

"Deal."

"What's the second thing?"

He looked confused, only for a moment, and then he nodded and reached for my hand. "When you're ready to tell your story, please tell it to me."

Something warm settled on my chest. "I will."

~

"What's all this for?" I asked Barbara as she unpacked a veritable mountain of eggs, flour, chocolate, butter, and all kinds of decorations.

"Upton's birthday," she said. "I always bake him a cake. Most of it goes to waste, but that's never stopped me before."

"His birthday?" I asked. "When is it?"

"Tomorrow."

I flexed my jaw. He never said a word to me. "He kept that quiet," I grumbled.

"He doesn't like any fuss," Barbara stated. "Not even before the accident. Jenna used to force him to celebrate, but it was always under duress." She made a sad face. "He never could say no to that poor girl."

An idea formed in my mind. "Barbara, would it be too much trouble if I asked you to make a very small cake for his actual birthday and then a much larger one for Saturday?"

Her eyes twinkled. "What are you planning?"

I drummed my fingers on the kitchen countertop and

leaned in conspiratorially. "He's going to celebrate this birthday whether he likes it or not, with people who love him and have missed him."

Barbara lit up from the inside out. "A dinner party? For how many?"

"I'll let you know. I just need to make a phone call."

I ducked outside and went to sit in my car—or rather, the car Upton loaned me. He had a habit of sneaking up on me, and the last thing I wanted was for him to overhear this conversation and try to derail it before I'd put the wheels in motion. I checked my watch. London was eight hours ahead, which put it at nine in the evening. Hopefully Sebastian wasn't an early to bed kind of guy.

He answered my call on the third ring and, lucky for me, sounded alert, if a little concerned. During my time in this job, I'd only called him twice, and on both occasions, I'd made sure the calls were during his working hours.

"Izabelle. Everything okay?"

"Yeah, great. Sorry to call you so late. Is this a bad time?"

"Not at all. What do you need?"

"I just found out it's Upton's birthday tomorrow, and the sneaky so-and-so kept it from me."

Sebastian chuckled. "He's not a huge celebrator of his birthday."

"So Barbara tells me. Except this year, I've decided things will be different."

Another chuckle. "You're settling in well, then?"

"Let's just say he's stopped trying to make me quit."

"Excellent. So, what's the plan?"

"Can you round up all his friends and see if they can come here, to his house, for a dinner party on Saturday evening?"

"Ohhh," Sebastian said, openly laughing now. "He'll hate every second."

"Too bad," I said. "I'm dragging him back into the land of

the living, whatever he says. He's ready. He's stubborn, that's all."

"I hope you know what you're doing."

"You leave him to me. So, can you arrange it with the others?"

"Yes. Oh, you'll need to cater for Oliver's kids."

"Great. The more the merrier. How many, and what ages?"

"Two. Nine and ten. Neither of them is particularly fussy, though, so I wouldn't worry too much."

"Got it," I said. "Shall we say six, that way it isn't too late for the children?"

"We'll be there."

I hung up and grinned to myself.

Welcome back to the world, Upton Barrick.

16

Upton

I paced across my bedroom, wearing out a track in the carpet. Belle had given me strict instructions to wait here for her until she came to fetch me. A surprise, she'd said.

I flexed my fingers to try to keep the pins and needles at bay. I hated surprises.

But for her, I complied. She'd been so excited when she disappeared thirty minutes ago with a final directive to wear a suit. I hadn't worn a suit since... Christ, since before the bomb. It felt weird, and I kept running my finger around the shirt collar. These days I preferred T-shirts or polos.

I'd already guessed what she had planned. She'd let me know in no uncertain terms how annoyed she was that I'd kept my birthday from her, and I'd seen her and Barbara with their heads together several times this week, plotting. She'd clearly asked Barbara to cook us a special birthday meal. I wasn't one for celebrating my birthday, not even before I lost Jenna—

although she'd pushed me into it year after year—and now it appeared as if Belle would be just as pushy.

If it made her happy, though, I'd give in. Go along with her wishes.

Fuck. She'd whipped me into shape, and I hadn't even seen it coming.

I wandered over to the window, smiling as I recalled watching her swim laps in the pool. I'd wanted nothing more than for her to quit back then, even if that hadn't stopped me jerking off to the sight of her in that tiny yellow bikini. I really must ask her for a second viewing.

"Ready?"

I spun around, and my jaw slackened. "Wow. You look... I mean... Jesus."

She smiled. "I hope the ends to these sentences are positive ones."

Belle had slithered her amazing, athletic body into a plum-colored fitted dress that clung to every curve and showed off a cleavage I wanted to bury my head between and happily take my last breath in. She'd put her hair up which showed off the creamy skin of her neck, and a silver pendant hung between her breasts. Her makeup was light and fresh. Perfect.

"C'mere," I said, although I walked toward her and she met me halfway. I circled her waist, running my hands over her hips, then tugged her closer. "Whatever you had planned, let's ditch it and make out instead."

I cut off her giggle, kissing her, tasting her, ruining her carefully applied lipstick. Heat licked through my veins as we went from zero to one hundred in a matter of seconds. A rumble of a moan sounded in her throat, and she burrowed beneath my jacket, the warmth from her hands seeping through my crisp white shirt.

Breaking off the kiss, I pressed my nose to her neck, breathing in the faint scent of a floral perfume, a subtle addition to the smell of her own skin rather than a detraction from it. This woman… she had class written all over her. The riches I'd amassed over the years, and the circles I'd moved in before I'd withdrawn from public life had meant I'd come into contact with all manner of the elite, and I knew with absolute certainty that Izabelle Laker had more class in her pinky than a lot of the nouveau riche I'd had to rub shoulders with over the years. Not only that, but she was kind, considerate, beautiful, funny, patient, and stubborn as fuck, given she was still here after I'd tried everything to make her quit in the early days.

I tucked a stray lock of hair that had escaped a bobby pin behind her ear. "I smudged your lipstick."

She cupped my cheek—the scarred one—and instead of jerking away, I leaned into her like a cat seeking attention.

"It's easily reapplied."

"I wouldn't bother," I said. "We'll be joined at the mouth for most of this evening anyway."

She brushed her thumb over my bottom lip.

I captured her wrist and bit the pad, then drew it into my mouth, sucking lightly. "Stop," she groaned. "We have to go."

I frowned, and then my stomach jolted as a thought occurred to me. "You haven't booked a restaurant, have you? I'm not in the mood for playing the part of circus freak this evening."

Her jaw tightened, and her eyes flashed with annoyance. "You are *not* a fucking circus freak," she snapped, surprising me with a rare curse. "No, I haven't booked a restaurant, but even if I had, we *would* go and you *would* enjoy yourself."

A shiver of pleasure traveled up my spine. I kind of liked Belle ordering me about. And I told her exactly that, which she laughed at.

"Zak is always telling me I'm bossy."

"He's not wrong."

She slipped her hand into mine and, together, we walked

downstairs. Turning right, we passed by the library and on down the hall to the formal dining room. She stopped outside and drew in a deep breath, almost as if she had to steel herself before entering.

"Don't be mad," she said, and before I could ask her what she meant, she opened the door and pushed me inside.

"Surprise!"

My eyes widened, and I looked around the room and then back at Belle, who stood a little off to my right, a demure smile touching lips still devoid of lipstick.

"Happy birthday, you old fucker," Sebastian said, pulling me into a hug. "Thirty-two. That's positively ancient."

"What's going on?" I asked as each of my friends stepped forward to shake my hand or, in the case of their wives and girlfriends, kiss my cheek. I accepted their affection in a kind of daze, whereas normally, I'd have backed away.

"It was Izabelle's idea," Sebastian said. "She called me earlier this week and asked if we'd come to LA to celebrate with you."

"I don't celebrate my birthday," I mumbled, and only then did I notice Zak sitting at the far end in the motorized wheelchair Belle had bought for him. A kinship I hadn't expected flowed between us, and when a broad smile etched across his face, so reminiscent of Belle's, I strode over and shook his hand.

"Great of you to come," I said.

Zak chuckled. "You should know my sister by now. Force of nature, that one. There's hardly any point arguing when she's set her mind on something."

"How well you know me, little brother," Belle said as she joined me. She slipped her arm through mine and smiled down at Zak.

"Less of the little," he said. "I can still best you, sis, even from this chair."

"Where's your Mom?" I asked Belle.

"Unfortunately, she couldn't get time off work. She's sorry she can't be here, though."

"That's a shame." I rather liked Belle's Mom, even though I'd only met her the one time. "Do you know everyone, Zak?"

"Yeah. We've been here for about an hour," Zak said. "We were under strict instructions not to make a sound, so, as you can imagine, we hardly dared to breathe."

"You are such a jerk, Zak," Belle said with a roll of her eyes.

As soon as we were all seated, Barbara came in with an appetizer of smoked salmon and cream cheese rolls with a spinach side salad. She squeezed my shoulder as she set down my plate, and I glanced up at her. "You're fired."

She laughed, reading me like a book. I'd never fire Barbara. The only way she'd leave my employment would be if it were her choice. She kissed my cheek, then whispered in my ear, "I've missed your smile."

Something warm and hazy appeared in my chest, and my eye caught Belle's. She pressed her hand to my thigh.

"Welcome back," she said, her tone low enough so that only I could hear.

And it hit me. Right there in the middle of my dining room, surrounded by my best friends and a woman who'd become so special to me.

I'd stopped feeling sad.

If someone held a gun to my head and asked me to pinpoint the exact date and time it had happened, I couldn't answer. But facts were facts.

Jenna would kick my ass from here to the beach and back again if she could. She'd have hated the man I'd become, so bitter and filled with guilt, cutting myself off from those who loved and cared for me. I mean, sure, Dad still treated me like a leper, and I was pretty certain Jenice spent her evenings wishing I'd died instead of Jenna—not on her own there—but I *had* survived. As much as I wished that it was the other way around and my little sister was here, I couldn't bring her back. I did, however, owe it to her to live my life to the fullest.

In front of all my friends, I eased up Belle's chin and kissed her. The room fell silent, and I knew without looking that every pair of eyes were on us—including Oliver's daughters, Annie, and Patsy, who he and Harlow, his girlfriend, had recently adopted—but I didn't care.

Someone cleared their throat, and I slowly withdrew from Belle's tantalizing and addictive lips.

"Well," she breathed. "That's one way to tell your friends you've corrupted your employee."

My eyes dropped to her cleavage. "I hope that one day soon, she'll allow me to corrupt her a little more."

I scanned the room and, confronted with a sea of faces, some stunned, some surprised, I shrugged. "What? Never seen a man kiss his girlfriend before?"

Belle stiffened beside me, and I covered the hand she'd left on my thigh with my own and wrapped my fingers around hers. Probably not the right place to announce that, but really, what other word for her was there?

After the first flush of surprise passed, I locked eyes with Garen. He nodded, a smile edging across his face, then slung his arm around his girlfriend, Catriona's, shoulders and kissed her temple.

We demolished the first course, something which pleased Barbara when she bustled into the room to clear away the plates. The entrée smelled just as fantastic and as everyone tucked in, the conversation thankfully moved away from me and Belle at the center of it.

I should have known the guys wouldn't be able to stay off the subject of work for very long, and despite Athena, Ryker's heavily pregnant wife berating him, he couldn't resist giving me a quick update and asking, bluntly, when I planned to return to work. I avoided giving him a direct answer, but the idea definitely appealed to me far more than it had at any time since that fateful night.

I shot the occasional glance Zak's way just to make sure he wasn't feeling left out or ostracized in any way, but each time I did, I found him deep in conversation with either Oliver to his right or Elliot to his left. He smiled when he caught my eye, then bent his head toward Elliot, nodding at something he said.

Only then did it occur to me that, apart from Zak, the only man here without a woman by his side was Sebastian. My best friend, wingman, and online gaming partner—although we hadn't done much of that lately, an issue I planned to put right very soon. A heaviness settled on my chest. Poor bastard. He deserved more.

As if he realized my thoughts had turned to him, he lifted his head and met my gaze. His eyes went to Belle, then back to me, and his lips curved up at the edges. He mouthed "Good choice".

Yeah. She was.

17

Belle

The evening was going perfectly. I couldn't have wished for a better night, or for a more favorable response from Upton. I'd taken a risk, for sure, but it had paid off—thank goodness. That all these men had shifted their schedules around so they could be here for Upton this evening should tell him everything he needed to know: he was surrounded by more love in this one room than most people received in a lifetime.

He'd stunned me when he'd announced to the entire room that I was his girlfriend, but I guessed, in truth, that's what I was. Ours wasn't a conventional relationship, beginning as it had with me as his employee. Upton's psychological challenges were still there—as were my own, hidden beneath the surface—but just looking at him tonight, chatting and laughing with his five best friends and their partners, I'd say his main troubles were behind him.

All I had to do now was to persuade him to get back out there. People might stare—I'd spent enough time with Zak to know that the world was full of rude assholes—but only by rejoining the human race would he learn to stand tall, eyes forward, and ignore those kinds of individuals. They didn't matter. That wasn't to say their blatant gawking and loud-enough-to-hear whispers wouldn't hurt, but the only way to learn to rise above their small-mindedness was to be the bigger person. To live your life as best you could.

I caught Zak's eye and smiled. He winked, then continued his conversation with Oliver, their dark heads close together as they chatted. My gaze continued around the table, eventually alighting on Brienna, Elliot's girlfriend. She looked glum and kept lowering her eyes and fiddling with the hem of her dress. Occasionally he'd whisper something to her, and she'd offer him a tight smile and a couple of words, then fall silent once more.

Wonder what her issue is?

I tried to grab her attention, to offer a little solidarity, but if she felt my stare, she ignored it.

"When are you due?" I asked Athena who was sitting across the table from me.

She rubbed her stomach, a wistful smile edging across her face. "Two weeks. Can't come quick enough now."

"Do you know what you're having?"

She shook her head. "Ryker didn't want to know. As long as it's healthy, I honestly don't care what we're having. I'm more worried about the birth itself. I've already told my doctors to line up all the drugs." She laughed.

Ryker cut his gaze to her, his eyes filled with the sort of adoration every woman craved. "I'll be right there, Thea." He placed his hand over the top of hers and kissed her temple. "And I promise I'll try not to faint."

"Helpful," she drawled, but her eyes said it all. There was a couple madly in love.

The conversation stilled as Barbara came into the dining

room carrying an enormous, two-tiered chocolate cake covered in candles. Oliver's daughter, Annie, could barely contain her excitement, and she nudged her sister, Patsy, almost salivating at the idea of stuffing their faces with the sugary treat.

"Daddy, look at that," Annie exclaimed. "I want a *huge* piece."

"Is that so?" Oliver tugged on her ponytail. "Well, as it's Uncle Upton's cake and not yours, you'll have to ask him if he's willing to share."

Annie pouted and then turned her attention to Upton. "But he can't eat all that by himself. He'll be sick."

Upton chuckled, leaning back to give Barbara enough room to set the cake down in front of him. "You can share with me, Annie bear, as soon as I've blown out the candles."

He did, and then we sang *Happy Birthday*, much to his chagrin, but he endured it without grumbling too loudly.

The conversation fell to a low hum as we ate dessert. Annie wolfed down her cake despite Oliver's best efforts to slow her down. Patsy ate hers much slower, savoring every mouthful, her eyes falling shut each time her lips closed around the spoon.

Annie pushed her plate to the side and then twisted in her seat toward Zak. "Why are you in that chair?" she asked, an innocent enough question for a child of her age. "Is there something wrong with your legs?"

Oliver looked horrified. "Annie Ellis!" he exclaimed. "Apologize right this second."

Zak smiled and motioned with his hand to show Oliver he wasn't remotely offended. "It's all cool," he said, turning his attention to Annie. "There's nothing wrong with my legs," he explained. "It's the communication from my brain to tell my legs to work, that's the problem. I hurt my back, and so the message isn't getting through, and that's why my legs have forgotten how to move."

"Oh." She leaned her head to the side, studying him. "How did you hurt your back?"

"Well," Zak said. "I went to watch a band play, about fifteen months ago now, and a bad man wanted to hurt us. He set off a bomb, and I got hurt."

Upton sucked in a breath, his gaze pinging between me and Zak.

And then he put two and two together.

"He was there?" he whispered in my ear. "The same concert?"

I nodded. *Shit.* I should have anticipated this coming up tonight, but I'd been so excited planning everything, it hadn't occurred to me. I'd meant to tell him, eventually. My intentions to keep it from him were honorable, but, too late, I realized my mistake. And now, the cat wasn't just out of the bag—it'd peed all over the table.

"And you didn't think to tell me? You didn't think that piece of information was important for me to know?"

The tone of his voice hardened, as did his eyes. Two amber orbs filled with hurt that I'd kept something so huge a secret.

"I wanted to," I stammered. "It just never felt like the right time."

Upton pushed his chair back and shot to his feet. He dabbed a napkin to the corners of his mouth, then threw it on top of his half-finished birthday cake. "Excuse me," he said to no one in particular.

I scrambled to follow him. Damn, he walked fast. "Upton," I called to his retreating back. "Wait."

I broke into a run, and then someone clasped my arm. Sebastian.

"Leave him for a while," he said. "I take it he didn't know your brother suffered his injuries at the same concert?"

I shook my head.

"Ah. Maybe you should have mentioned it before tonight."

"That's not the half of it," I muttered.

"Oh? Care to elaborate?"

I dug my fingertips into my temple to stave off an impending tension headache, then blew out a slow breath through pursed lips. "Not really."

Sebastian grinned, then put his arm around my shoulder. "Come on, I happen to know where Upton keeps the good brandy. You look like you could do with one."

I allowed him to chivvy me along. We ended up in the library. Sebastian went straight to a cabinet in the corner and crouched, returning to his feet holding two crystal glasses in one hand and a bottle in the other. He set the glasses down and poured two healthy portions, handing one of them to me.

"Thanks." I sipped, the liquid burning my throat, but it did halt the wobble in my legs.

"You should take it as a compliment that he got a little pissy," Sebastian said. "It shows that he gives a shit about you."

I smiled faintly. "I'd rather have gotten through the evening without upsetting him. It'd all gone so well. Maybe I shouldn't have invited Zak. It's just he doesn't get out as much as I'd like, and he and Upton really hit it off when they met, and I wanted to do something nice for them both." I allowed my legs to buckle and sank into a nearby chair.

Sebastian perched on the edge of the adjacent couch. "And you did. We haven't all sat around together since before Upton's accident. We've tried. Believe me. Yet where every single one of us failed to reach him, you succeeded. Don't underestimate how much of an achievement that is." He took a deep swallow of his drink. "I remember saying to Garen after your interview that I had a good feeling about you. And I love being right. It feeds my ego. Looks as if you've earned that large bonus nine months ahead of schedule."

I chuckled despite the weight of regret pressing heavily on my chest.

"He'll get over his hissy fit in no time," Sebastian continued. "He'll just want to know why you didn't tell him about Zak. I must admit, it's interesting that you invited your brother, even if you did want him to get out more. You must have considered the possibility of questions, especially knowing kids would be here. In my experience, children aren't usually backward in coming forward."

"I didn't," I confessed. "I honestly didn't."

But was that true? Maybe my subconscious had forced me into this position. I'd been struggling for a while about how to tell Upton of our intertwined pasts. Perhaps this was my subconscious mind's way of forcing the issue.

"Zak isn't the only thing I kept from him," I said, my head bowed. I set the drink on a nearby end table and rubbed my forehead. "God, this is all such a mess."

Sebastian leaned forward, curiosity swimming in his slate-gray eyes. "We might not know each other very well, but I'm a good listener if you want to talk." He laughed. "Actually, that's a lie. I'm a terrible listener, but I'll do my best."

My smile came slow and didn't last. "I was supposed to go to that concert with my fiancé. I got caught up at work and couldn't get away in time, so I asked Zak if he'd go with Marin. They got along really well, and he was happy to do it." I covered my face with my hands as pain filled my chest, squishing my lungs, and making it difficult to take a full breath.

"What happened to your fiancé?" Sebastian asked gently.

"He died." My voice came out all muffled, but I couldn't seem to remove my hands from my face, almost as if I was hiding my shame. "It should have been me. If I'd gone like I was supposed to, then Marin might be alive and Zak wouldn't be paralyzed."

A sob crawled into my throat, but I forced it back down. Tears did nothing. I'd shed enough to fill a bathtub, but not a single one brought Marin back or gave Zak the use of his legs.

Silence filled the room, the only sound Sebastian's steady breathing.

Finally, he spoke. "Well, aren't you two quite the pair?"

I dropped my hands and met his gaze. "We have more in common than most, yeah."

"And yet you've never told him any of this, have you?"

I shook my head, then pointlessly added, "No."

"Why not? Why tell me and not him?"

"Yes, Izabelle," a cold voice filled with bitterness said from behind me. "Do share."

18

Upton

Belle's head snapped in my direction, and her neck and cheeks flushed with color. I hardly spared her a glance, instead locking my gaze on Sebastian.

"Get out," I snapped.

He immediately rose to his feet and ambled across the room, unperturbed by my foul mood. As he passed, he patted me on the shoulder. "Go easy, yeah?"

I ignored him, waiting until he'd crossed the threshold, then I kicked the door closed with the heel of my shoe. Seconds scraped by with neither of us speaking. Belle kept her eyes trained on one of the enormous floor-to-ceiling bookcases that spanned an entire wall in my library, filled with books I'd never read but aspired to own anyway. First editions, classics, thrillers, crime novels, and even the odd young adult romance book purchased for Jenna to read when she came over for a visit.

Might as well donate those to a local bookstore now.

What the fuck am I musing about romance novels for?

I crossed the room and helped myself to a glass of single malt imported from Scotland. They distilled the best whisky in my opinion, and I had it shipped over from the UK by the case. It wasn't as if the enormous transportation costs made even a dent in my bank balance.

"Upton, I—"

"Why did you tell him and not me?" I kept my back to her, studying the amber liquid, almost the same color as my eyes, sloshing up the sides of the glass as I twisted it in my hands. "I knew there was something, and after our picnic, I asked you to talk to me when you were ready. You agreed, yet you decided to tell Sebastian instead, a man you hardly know."

"It just came out."

I set down the glass and turned around slowly, jealousy roaring through my veins. She told Sebastian. *Sebastian.* I glued my hands to my sides. If I didn't anchor them there, I'd smash one or both right through the drywall, and I refused to show her how much her betrayal hurt like a motherfucker.

Every day, for *months,* she'd arrived at my house, all the while knowing that she and I had so much in common and yet she'd chosen to stay silent, as if it was a dirty little secret that mustn't ever be mentioned. I'd given her so many opportunities to talk to me, shared my own hurt and anger over losing my father, and what Jenna's death had done to me, and yet she'd still played her cards close to her chest.

Until tonight.

And she hadn't opened up to me. No, she'd bestowed that gift on my best friend instead.

"I thought we had something."

She leaped to her feet, her arms stretching toward me in a pleading manner. "We do. We do have something."

I snorted. "No, we don't. We can't have. All this time... *all this time,* Belle, the hours we sat on the patio talking and laughing.

The conversation we had about my father, the things I shared with you about Jenna, and yet you failed to mention *anything* about your links to the concert that killed my sister, killed *your* fiancé, ruined my face, left me with a back full of scars, and stole the ability for your brother to ever walk again. And then one brief chat with Sebastian and you're spilling your guts to him when you couldn't to me. Tell me, does that sound like we have anything to you? Anything at all?"

"Please," she begged. "Just listen to me."

I flexed my jaw, grinding my molars loud enough that she had to be able to hear them. I almost walked out. Almost. But in the end, I wanted to see how she wormed her way out of this. I picked up my half-finished glass of whisky and took a seat, one about as far away from her as I could get. Crossing my right ankle over my left knee, I stretched my arm along the back of the couch and gestured to her with my drink. "I'm listening."

She swept a hand down her face then, with a heavy sigh, chose to sit in the chair, the message from my stiff body language hitting its mark.

"When I first started working here, I had no intention of telling you anything about me. I had a job to do, and I was going to do it to the best of my ability. My personal life was none of your business. And then, as you warmed to me, or at least stopped trying to make me quit, I realized that I wanted you to accept me for me, not because our lives were connected in the most horrifying of ways. Our experiences are too similar, Upton. And so I made the decision not to tell you. To have you come around on your own, and not because you felt some kind of kinship because we both lost someone we loved at the same event."

"That's a ridiculous reason," I scoffed.

"No, it isn't." She scraped a hand through her hair, tugging out several strands that fell onto the arm of the chair. "After it happened, I received so many messages from other victims.

Some, like me, weren't there, but had family who were. Other messages from those who were injured themselves. They wanted to reach out, to form connections with someone they felt understood them. But I didn't want to surround myself with horrific reminders. I didn't want my head full of their stories. I had enough trouble managing my own. And when I got this job, and I met you… you were so broken. All I wanted was to fix you, but I wanted to do that without you knowing that when I said I understood what you were feeling, I really meant it. It wasn't just words, but spoken from a place of empathy. Only those who went through what we did can truly understand."

"That still doesn't explain why you found it so easy to tell Sebastian and not me."

She shook her head and pinched the bridge of her nose. "The longer I kept it from you, the harder I found it to confess. Something Sebastian said made me think that there's a possibility on some level that I invited Zak to force the conversation, but…" Her voice trailed off, and her chin lowered to her chest. She nibbled on her thumbnail, her focus absolute.

"Perhaps it's Sebastian you want, not me," I said bitterly.

"Don't be ridiculous," she snapped.

"Ridiculous? Is it?" I hit back, completely lost now to the green-eyed monster. "If it was so easy to tell him and not the man you've been tangling tongues with for weeks, then maybe he's the one you want. Although I should warn you that he's in love with his brother's girlfriend, and so you might have a hell of a job of trying to divert his attention. Still, worth a shot, yeah? Bag yourself a perfect billionaire rather than one who's as fucked-up as me."

Her jaw dropped, and she gave a slow, disbelieving headshake. "How could you?" she gritted out. "Do you think so little of me?"

I shrugged. "If the boot fits."

Color drained from her face, and her body seemed to

crumple in on itself. She unsteadily got to her feet. "If that's what you really think, then there's nothing more to say," she whispered.

She smoothed a hand over her abdomen and walked away, her shoulders bowed, spine curved.

As if I'd been in some kind of trance, I came to, horrified at the words I'd spoken.

What the fuck are you doing? Don't let her leave. Not like this. Not over something that's eminently fixable.

The opening of the door propelled me to my feet. I reached her in one second and slammed it shut, then planted my hands on either side of her head. I buried my nose in her hair and breathed in the scent of her shampoo. Peaches. Whenever I thought of Belle, peaches always came to mind, the smell of the sweet fruit in her hair, on her skin.

"Don't go."

She turned around slowly, hurt swirling in her green irises, darkened and dull rather than vibrant and full of life. "You hurt me."

My chest throbbed with pain, and I hung my head. "I know."

"Did you mean it?"

"No."

"Then why say it?"

Shame flooded me. "I was jealous," I admitted.

Her eyes glistened, and she'd never looked more beautiful. "Oh, Upton."

God, I want her. Right here, right now, despite a room full of guests down the hall.

I crashed my mouth on hers, my kiss tinged with a combination of punishment and apology. My hips pinned her to the door, trapping her in place. If she wanted to escape now, too bad.

Her arms snaked around my shoulders, her fingertips

playing with the hair at my nape. Earlier, I'd lost myself to jealousy. Now, I was lost in a haze of passion and raw, unbridled need. My hands clawed at the hem of her dress, almost as if they belonged to another. I broke off the kiss only to allow me to hurriedly unzip it, and it dropped in a pool of material at her feet. And then I was right back on her, drinking from her as if I needed this to survive.

Maybe I did.

I unclasped her bra with one hand and slipped my other inside her panties, groaning at what I found there. Heat, so much heat. And wet, soaked, just for me. I pushed one finger inside her, quickly following up with another. She rocked her hips, riding my hand, our noisy breaths mingling together.

Flicking open the button on my trousers, I reached inside and freed my dick. Damn, I was ready to blow before I got anywhere near her pussy. I tried to think of other things, less sexy things, but my mind wouldn't stay there. Surrounded by the smell, the taste, the feel of a woman after so long, and one I'd dreamed for weeks of fucking, had me raising her. I hooked her thighs around my waist, shoved her panties to one side, and lined up my cock with her entrance. One push forward, and I was balls deep.

"God, fuck, you're tight."

I didn't wait for a reply, kissing her again, my tongue thrusts keeping time with my hips. My thighs trembled from excitement and the strain of holding her up. I withdrew, then slammed into her over and over and over. She clung to me, meeting me every inch of the way. Using the door to take some of the strain, I cupped her breast and, somehow, managed to lift the erect nipple to my mouth. When I sucked, she cried out, and her pussy clenched around me.

"God, do that again," I begged.

She did, and my balls tightened in response. I shifted my position so that every push forward, my groin rubbed her clit.

That friction coupled with the attention I gave her nipple had her peaking in seconds, the culmination of weeks of sexual tension. She toppled over into climax, her muscles pulsing against my cock, the sounds of her cries in my ear.

"Ah, fuck," I ground out, my cum spilling inside her, my dick jerking with a long-forgotten pleasure that made me feel as if every muscle I possessed had been taken from me. My legs shook as I eased her down to the floor.

The passion that had exploded out of me receded, and common sense came flooding back.

Shit. No condom.

I shoved my dick back inside my pants and zipped up. "Fuck, Belle, I'm sorry."

A crease appeared between her eyebrows, and I wanted to kiss it away.

"For what?"

I grazed my teeth over my bottom lip. "I didn't use a condom."

She nodded, then chuckled. "I know. Your sperm is trickling down my legs."

"But what if...?"

"I get pregnant?" she asked, her brow arched. "I won't. I'm on birth control. Unless it's STIs you were worried about. In which case I'd say pregnancy was more likely given our particular circumstances, wouldn't you?"

She had a point, but still...

"Stay there," I muttered. "I'll get you a cloth."

I darted into the guest bath, praying it wasn't in use. I got lucky. In less than a minute, I'd returned to the library. I handed over the damp cloth, averting my eyes while she cleaned herself up. I should say something, but I didn't know what to say. We hadn't exactly planned this. Then again, in my experience, the best sex was usually unplanned.

And that… that had been right up there with fucking awesome sex, despite only lasting minutes.

Next time, I'd do better.

"What are you thinking?" Belle asked, standing before me now, fully dressed.

I reached for her hand and pulled her to me. "That we need to do that again, and this time I'm going to savor you for hours."

19

Belle

Upton towed me back to the dining room, and all I could think was, "I hope they can't smell sex on me."

I'd cleaned up the best I could, but every now and then, I caught a hint of my arousal mingled with his.

And I wouldn't change a thing.

Well, apart from the timing. Maybe. But the spontaneity of it had been exactly what we'd both needed, especially after I'd screwed up so badly by telling Sebastian my secret before I'd shared it with Upton. He could have cut me off entirely, yet in the end, his anger and betrayal were the things that had brought us together. Our relationship had progressed these past few weeks, but then it had kind of stalled after the trip up the mountain, almost as if we hadn't known how to take that next step, and so we'd teetered on the edge, moving neither forward nor backward.

We entered the dining room, and the hum of conversation stopped. Sebastian's gaze went to where our hands were joined, and a smile tugged at the corners of his mouth. His eyes collided with mine, and he inclined his head. I think that was his way of extending his approval.

"It was great to see you all," Upton announced. "But Belle and I have a few things to discuss, and so we'll leave you to it." He turned to go, then stopped and faced the table once more. "You guys all have hotel rooms, right? Or did you need to stay here?"

"We're good," Ryker drawled. "But thanks for the latent thought of hospitality."

Upton shot a glare at Ryker who just grinned.

"Zak," I began, but Upton was way ahead of me.

"Zak, you're welcome to stay. There's a room on the ground floor that Barbara can easily make up for you, or if you'd rather go home, one of the guys will make sure you get there safely."

Zak sought me out, his smile exuding happiness. "I'll stay if that's okay. It'd be good to catch up with my sister over breakfast." He finished off with a wink.

I sent a glower in his direction.

"Actually, that's a great idea, Zak," Sebastian said. "I say we all meet here for breakfast in the morning. Around nine?"

Upton glanced down at me, his golden eyes burning, and making me burn, too.

"Make it ten," he said.

Sebastian barked out a laugh. "Ten it is."

We escaped upstairs, Upton's long strides meaning I had to do the occasional skip to keep up with him. He led me into his bedroom, closing the door behind me. I held my breath, anticipating a fast come-on, given what had happened in the library. Instead, he crossed over to the window, drew the drapes, and then turned around and raked his gaze over me, head to foot and back again.

"Come here," he murmured. "I went too fast before. This

time, I want to relish you. To touch and kiss every inch of you. And afterward, we're going to talk."

I caught the hint of steel in his tone at the talking part. *You're not out of the woods yet, Belle.* He mustn't have bought my reasoning of why I'd shared details with Sebastian instead of him, and I wasn't sure I had any more satisfactory answers. Sebastian was warm and funny whereas Upton was surly and spent a lot of time brooding, and I could just imagine how it would go down if I offered that up as an explanation. Besides, that wasn't the reason. I'd made an honest mistake, that was all.

Then again, Upton wasn't nearly as sullen and moody these days. He definitely smiled more, although he could still disappear inside his head on occasion, making him impossible to reach.

"I'm waiting."

Smiling at his not-so-subtle command, I kicked off my shoes and padded over to him, curling my toes in his deep-pile wall-to-wall carpeting. He flicked my hair over one shoulder, his fingertips brushing my neck as he did so. I shivered from his touch.

His gaze rested on my face. "You saved me," he murmured, his hand curling around the back of my neck to the nape.

He massaged gently, and tingles shot down my arms and legs. I closed my eyes, savoring the feel of him, the smell of him, soon, I hoped, the taste of him.

"We saved each other," I replied. "You might not believe me, but I needed you almost as much as you needed me."

The pad of his thumb caressed my earlobe, and my stomach tied itself in knots. God, he meant it when he said he planned to take his time. He'd hardly touched me, and already I was a hot mess.

He inched my zipper down, slowly, building the anticipation. I parted my lips, inviting him to kiss me. He ignored my open invitation, instead his fingertips and his thumb continued to explore the soft skin on my neck, my earlobe, my cheek, almost as if he was a blind man trying to memorize my face through touch alone.

And all the while his amber eyes burned—and I went up in flames.

My dress came loose and then fell in a heap at my feet. Only then did his eyes leave my face, and his hands followed, touching first my collarbone then heading south where he cupped my right breast through my lace bra. My nipple hardened instantly.

"You're too beautiful for me," he muttered. "But I don't care. I'm stealing you anyway."

I thought about arguing, of telling him—again—that his scars only enhanced his appeal rather than detracted from his insanely good looks, but I'd be wasting my breath. Upton still needed more time to reconcile what he felt he'd lost with the reality. He truly believed his attractiveness only came down to his physical appearance. He failed, yet, to see the full picture. He would. Eventually.

"Can I undress you?" I asked, the flat of my palm connecting with his taut, broad chest.

He swallowed and nodded.

I slipped my hands beneath his jacket, up over his shoulders, and slid it down his arms. When I bent to pick it up—even I knew an expensive suit when I saw one—he stopped me with a firm grip on my arm and a shake of his head.

"Leave it."

My fingers slowly unfastened the buttons on his shirt, and I prayed I wouldn't fumble. I'd only seen him naked from the waist up once, and the sight of him had filled my dreams for days. Now I'd not only get to see him naked, but to touch him as well. Explore his body with my hands and my lips and my tongue.

His shirt joined the jacket, and I went to work on his

trousers. He stepped out of them and stood before me, all ropes of muscle and tanned skin. I dropped my gaze. He already had an erection, the head peeking out from the top of his black boxers. I had no idea what made me do it. With little experience to call upon, I was acting on instinct alone. And that instinct sent me to my knees. I stared up at him, waiting for him to say something, or guide me, or maybe even stop me.

He did none of those things.

Instead, with hooded eyes, he loomed over me, his throat working, his jaw tight, his thighs locked in place.

I slipped my thumbs into his underwear and rolled his boxers down his legs. His cock sprang free, right at my eye level. Thick and long and hard.

No wonder I'd winced when he'd pushed inside me in the library.

I'd only ever seen one other—Marin's. And it didn't look like that.

Stop. Stay in the now.

The past was the past, and my immediate future was entangled with the stunning man standing naked before me. How long that'd last was anyone's guess. We, more than most, understood how things could change in the time it took someone to snap their fingers. Life was short, and whereas Upton had closed himself off in order to cope with his grief, I'd chosen to exorcise my guilt by being the best version of me I could be, and help others.

And I counted Upton as a success story.

"If you don't touch it or lick it or fucking suck it soon, I'm going to lose my ever-loving mind."

His words brought a smile to my face. I'd gotten lost in my thoughts for a moment, exactly like he did at times. I wondered what he thought of on those occasions when his eyes glazed over and he'd sit with Bandit in his lap, absentmindedly stroking him as he stared out across his backyard.

I must ask him one day.

But not now.

"Belle," he growled.

I flicked my tongue over the head, capturing the bead of moisture along his slit. He sucked in a sharp breath through his teeth, and his cock jerked.

"More."

I gripped the base and angled the head toward me, then closed my lips over him. The musky taste of man spilled onto my taste buds. He was steel wrapped in satin. Flawless.

His hands burrowed into my hair, but he didn't push, or pull, or tug. He simply anchored them there, almost as if he needed to steady himself. His thighs quivered, and when I swirled my tongue around him, his chest rumbled with a soft groan.

I lost myself to him, settling into a rhythm that he must have approved of if the sounds he made were any indication. I'd kept my gaze lowered, but as he thickened beneath my hand and my tongue and I sensed he was close, I risked a peek at him.

My clit throbbed. *Jesus, that's so damned hot.* He had his eyes closed, his full lips parted in a silent moan, his head leaning back. His abs rippled every time I pulled him deep, and his thighs shook so much, I wondered how they were holding him upright.

My free hand traveled over my stomach, and I touched myself. A jolt of electricity coursed through me, my orgasm on the brink from giving pleasure rather than receiving it.

That's new. And addictive. So very addictive.

"Make yourself come," Upton ground out, and only then did I realize he'd opened his eyes and was watching me, fascinated. "God, Belle, do it."

I groaned around him, my throat vibrating against his cock.

"Fuck."

His fingers tightened in my hair, and I rubbed the nub of

nerves between my parted thighs, sucking harder on him in response to my own approaching climax.

"Sweet fucking Jesus."

White spots danced before my eyes, and a swell, almost a convulsion, grew in my lower abdomen. I rubbed harder, faster, and in response, my other hand, the one wrapped around Upton's erection, sped up, too.

"Shit, damn."

His essence spilled onto the back of my tongue and slid down my throat. Seconds later, I peaked and tumbled over the edge. I released him, my head lolling back, a satisfied moan spilling from my lips.

I found myself encased in Upton's arms, and he held me close to his strong, taut chest, then set me down on top of the bed. He lay down beside me, and his warm palm skated up my side, and his lips claimed mine. I sank into his kiss, needing the moment to gather my thoughts after the intimacy of what we'd shared. Sex in the library had exploded with heat and passion and a raw intensity that we'd both needed in that moment. But this... this... I felt full and satisfied and cherished. Strange to think of oral sex in that way. I hadn't particularly enjoyed it on the few occasions I'd done it with Marin, but with Upton it not only felt new, but different.

Erotic.

Sensory overload.

His hands roved over me, and my bra and panties ended up tossed across the room. He settled between my thighs and cupped my face, his golden irises filled with an openness that made my heart soar.

I traced his scar with my fingertip. He flinched, but barely.

I called that progress.

20

UPTON

Soft lips, tender hands, the smell of peaches. Silken tresses caressing me. Fingertips touching, tracing between my shoulder blades. Firm, rounded breasts pressed to my back. A shapely leg thrown over mine.

This is the best dream ever.

I expelled a soft groan, wanting the pleasure to go on and on, but a part of me knew it wouldn't last. Nothing good lasted. Love and loss. Pain and suffering. Hurt and anger. Grief and guilt. As soon as I awoke, the depression and despair and dread at facing another day would return. Better to stay here, inside my dream, where I was whole and normal, and me.

The me I used to be before—

My eyes flickered open. A shard of sunlight peeked through the drapes where I hadn't closed them properly. I blinked, the remnants of my dream already fading before I could grasp on to the details, but whatever I'd dreamed about, the fragments of its warmth remained.

"Morning, handsome."

I twisted my head, greeted by Izabelle's easy-going smile and gentle eyes instead of an empty pillow or, occasionally, Bandit's awful dog breath. My insides twisted. She was so fucking gorgeous, even with just-woken mussed hair and mascara smudges where she'd failed to remove her makeup last night.

We never got around to having that talk.

Ah, fuck it. Sex first, conversation second.

"Hey." My voice rasped, still heavy with sleep. "What're you doing?"

She pressed a kiss to my back. "Exploring."

The sensation of her lips on my scars had me stiffening. I shuffled away and then rolled onto my back. I hooked an arm behind my head and forced my mouth to curl at the edges in an attempt to distract her. "You're welcome to explore my dick," I said, expecting her to laugh.

She didn't.

Instead, she paused for two or three seconds, let out a heavy sigh, then threw back the covers and got out of bed.

"Where are you going?" I rolled onto my side and propped up my head. "It was only a joke. Come back to bed." I'd gone to sleep last night dreaming of morning sex and woke up ready to fulfil the fantasy. I patted the mattress.

She turned her back to me, pulled on her panties, slipped her arms through the straps of her bra and fastened it, then spun around, hands planted on her hips and glared at me. "You know, for a smart man, you're an idiot."

I widened my eyes, genuinely stunned, struggling to catch up with the speed with which we'd gone from the heady heights of the morning after to this. And all because I made a dick joke?

"I'm a man. We make stupid jokes at inappropriate times. Don't judge me too harshly."

"Jesus, Upton. You don't get it, do you?"

I sat up, my temper rising at her refusal to explain what the fuck she was talking about. "Clearly I don't. Fucking hell, Belle. I never took you for the uptight kind."

Her eyes sent a burst of fire in my direction, all exasperation and barely suppressed rage. She snatched up her dress from the floor, creasing the material where she fisted it in her hands.

Hands that were shaking.

What the hell?

"I'm going home," she said, tugging on her dress.

I threw back the covers and sprang out of bed, reaching her just as she began the battle of trying to zip it up without assistance.

"Stop, Belle." I wrapped my hand around her wrist, preventing her from continuing. "Just stop. Tell me what's going on."

Slowly, doubt had trickled into my mind. This couldn't be over some mistimed dick joke. I'd missed a cue, something along the way that resulted in this... outburst.

"I kissed you, on your back, and you acted as if I'd given you a venereal disease. You couldn't move away fast enough."

"Oh, that." I shifted my gaze to the window.

"Yes, that." She palmed my shoulder to get my attention. "I don't want to have to second guess where I can and can't touch you, Upton."

I rubbed my fingertips over my lips. "I don't like being touched there."

"Why not?"

My eyebrows shot up. "Why not? That isn't a serious question, surely? Have you seen the fucking mess back there? The better question is why would you want to touch me, let alone kiss me, in that particular location. It's ruined and ugly. Why would you want to even look at it?"

She threw her hands in the air. "Jesus, Upton. Do you think so little of me?"

My head jerked back. "This isn't about you, Belle. It's about me."

"I disagree." She added a vigorous head shake to press home the extent of her vehemence. "You're imprinting your hang-ups on me. You think that because *you* have an issue with how your back looks, then that means *I* must have an awful aversion to your scars." She snorted. "For the avoidance of doubt, I don't. I want to kiss you and touch you. And I don't want to have to segment your body into sections either and then have to remember which bits are off limits. It's a total buzz kill, and I won't do it."

Her chest rose and fell, a sign of her frustration. Silent seconds inched by. I wanted to explain, or at least try to, but the words stuck in my throat. I had a difficult enough time allowing the nurses and doctors at the hospital to see the destruction the bomb had caused, how pieces of shrapnel and flying debris had torn through my skin and the muscle beneath with ease, leaving a path of devastation similar to the picture a three-year-old might create if you gave them a pen and a piece of paper and asked them to draw whatever came to mind.

"You know what? Forget it."

Belle made for the door, her zipper still only halfway up her back. Like an action replay of last night in the library, I tore after her, my palms hitting the door before she had a chance to fully open it. The slamming sound reverberated through the house, and I half expected Barbara to scuttle upstairs to make sure everything was okay.

I buried my nose in her hair. "Don't leave. Please. You've changed everything for me. I'm a different person since you came into my life, and damn, I don't want to regress to the lonely, cold, miserable asshole I was before." I said the latter hoping to bring the beginnings of a smile to her lips. But even from this angle where she faced the door, I could tell there was no smile.

"I can't do this," she whispered.

A cold rush of fear surged into my veins. I could feel her slipping away, like sand through cupped hands. No matter how hard you tried to hold on, those grains always escaped.

"Please. Just give me time. You're right. This is my hang-up, and it might take me a while, but you've made such a difference to my self-esteem, Belle. Don't give up on me. Not now. Not over this."

This entire time, she'd clasped the door handle. When she let go and slowly turned to face me, my knees buckled. And then I saw the tears in her eyes. Brimming. One spilled over, and then another.

"Jesus, fuck, please don't cry. I can't stand it."

"I'm sorry. God, I'm so sorry. What was I thinking?" She fisted her hair and tugged. "You're not the asshole. I am."

Stunned, I took a step back, my eyes wide. "What?"

"I'm the first woman to touch you there, yes?"

"Apart from my nurses, that's correct."

"And you react exactly as I'd expect you to, yet I get all pissy and territorial and yell at you for doing exactly what I expected."

She moved away from the door, and her hands came around my face. She brushed her thumb over my scar, and I barely flinched. I'd gotten used to her touching that particular injury, and it didn't bother me as much as it once had.

Rising onto her tiptoes, she pressed her lips to mine. "We'll take it slow. I promise."

"You're staying?" I rasped, realizing we'd had our first real-relationship fight.

"If you'll have me."

I mashed my lips to hers. "No question. Now come back to bed. I have plans."

Belle lay curled in my arms, tendrils of her hair tickling my face, but I didn't care. In fact, I nuzzled closer, smelling her shampoo, her skin, the faintest trace of the perfume she'd dabbed to her neck last night. Contentment sank into my bones. I felt lighter, expunged of the weight I often carried within me, albeit my demons had been in retreat for a while now.

"Tell me about your fiancé, about that night."

She stiffened in my arms, and I squeezed her tighter. Belle didn't have visible scars, like me, but there wasn't a doubt in my mind she carried very deep ones within her. "I want to know everything."

She sighed softly and snuggled in to me. "Marin loved Savage Groove's music. I used to tease him about it given they had quite the teenage girl following, but he didn't care. He liked what he liked. So, when I found out they were ending their world tour in LA, I bought us tickets. I remember how thrilled he was, counting down the days to the event."

She fell silent. I left her to her thoughts. This was her story, and it was important I allowed her to take her time, to tell it in her own way. She sighed again, and I tightened my arms around her. A way of showing moral support.

"That day, one of my elderly patients suffered a heart attack."

"You were a carer for the elderly, before me?" How had I not known this?

Because you never asked, you selfish bastard.

She nodded, unaware of the shard of guilt that sliced through my midriff. No wonder she'd never told me about that night and what she'd lost. Despite our growing familiarity over these last few weeks, the vast majority of the conversations had all been about me. Well that changed. Today.

"I'd worked in that sector since leaving school," she continued. "There's something very rewarding about looking after old people. It's a difficult job, especially when they get sick, or dementia sets in and you watch them fade before your very eyes, but I love listening to their stories and watching their eyes light up as they recall their pasts."

"Yet you gave it up for me," I murmured.

"The money Sebastian and Garen offered was too good to pass up. I knew the difference it would make to Zak and Mom. I plan to return, though."

"When you're done with me?"

She shifted her weight, rested her head on my chest, and placed her palm right over my heart. "I'm not sure I'll ever be done with you."

My chest tightened, and a thickness in my throat made it difficult to swallow. I twisted a lock of her hair and urged her to continue.

"Anyway, Marjorie, that's the lady who had the heart attack. She had no family, and she was so scared of going to the hospital. I remember her crying, saying once old people went in there they never came out. She begged me to go with her, to stay with her. I mean, I could hardly say no, and anyway, I didn't want to. Anyone would have felt the same."

She took in a huge breath, and I got the feeling we were approaching the heart of the story.

"So I called Zak and asked if he'd go with Marin to the concert."

Ah.

"That one decision changed so much," she whispered. "Marin died, Zak lost the use of his legs."

"That one decision also meant that you're here."

She shifted her gaze, meeting mine. "But at what cost? My life isn't worth more than theirs. I don't think I'll ever completely forgive myself, no matter how much time passes. I remember sitting beside Zak's bed sobbing, begging for forgiveness after we learned he'd never walk again, and all he did was pat my arm and tell me he loved me."

The contrast with my own family stole my breath. Dad had given up on me, choosing Jenice instead, and she... well, I was fairly sure if she ever saw me in the street, she'd either gun me down or run me over. Zak had forgiven Belle, but there would be no such compassion for me.

"What happened to Marjorie?"

"She died."

"Oh God, I'm sorry." I kissed the top of her head.

"In a way, her passing made it worse. If she'd lived, then it might have confirmed... oh, I don't know... that my decision had been the right one."

"Were you there? To the very end?"

I nodded. "I held her hand."

"Then your decision was the right one."

She twisted her lips to the side. "Yeah, maybe. But what I went through was the reason why I knew I was perfect for this job. As soon as I found out what had happened to you, I had to take the position. I guess, on some level, I thought that by helping you, I might find some peace for myself."

"And have you?"

She stayed quiet for the longest time, and I almost repeated the question until she whispered, "Yes, I think I have."

21

Belle

"You're awfully late," Sebastian said, making a point of looking at his watch as Upton and I entered the kitchen. "I mean, you must have gone to bed at what? Nine? Most of us have already eaten thanks to the marvel that is the beautiful Barbara." He rose to his feet and kissed Upton's housekeeper on the cheek. She blushed furiously. Then again, Sebastian was the epitome of charm.

"Fuck off, Seb," Upton growled.

I quickly checked around, relieved when I spotted Oliver and Harlow outside with the children. Kids their age picked up on *everything.*

"What would you two lovebirds like to eat?" Barbara asked.

Sebastian sniggered, earning another fierce glare from Upton.

"I'm fucking warning you. One more, and you're going in the pool. Fully dressed."

"Yeah, yeah." Sebastian snagged a piece of toast from a pile in the middle of the table. "Elliot had to fly back to New York. Some bullshit about a deal, but given the fight I witnessed between him and Brie last night, I'd say it had more to do with his crumbling relationship than ROGUES."

"She looked pretty glum at dinner," Upton said.

"Can you blame her?"

My interest piqued. I knew very little about Upton's coworkers or their other halves. Each snippet, from the one Upton mentioned in anger last night about Sebastian and his brother's girlfriend, and now Elliot's 'trouble in paradise', amplified my curiosity. They were an interesting bunch of people, that's for sure.

"Why?" I asked. "What's wrong?"

Upton poured two coffees and pushed one across to me, then cocked his head for us to go outside. He held up a hand in greeting to his friends, but then hung back to give me the briefest of updates while Sebastian went to join the group.

"Athena, Ryker's wife, is Elliot's sister. Almost four years ago, she was kidnapped, and they had to pay a hefty price to her abductor."

I gasped, but he continued.

"Since then, Elliot has grown increasingly..." he paused, searching for the right word, "frantic in his attempts to find the perpetrator. My guess is that his single-minded determination to bring the kidnapper to justice is affecting his relationship."

"Have they dated long?"

"Yeah. A long time. Even before Ryker and Athena got together." He pinched his nose. "None of us know what to do with him, to be honest. I've been out of it, as you know, but given what Sebastian said, and the body language I picked up on last night, I'd say Elliot's gotten worse, not better."

I slipped my arm through his. "Sounds like he could use a friend."

"Yeah, maybe. But if Ryker can't get through to him, no one

can. Those two have been tight since school. The rest of us met at college, but Ryker and Elliot grew up together."

"That's so sad," I said.

Upton bent to kiss me, but as his lips touched mine, Zak hollered, "Jesus, man, put her down," which the rest of the group responded to by whistling and catcalling.

"You're lucky there are kids present," Upton said as we approached.

Ryker pulled out a couple chairs. "Sit your asses down. We have things to discuss."

Upton set his cup on the table and shifted the chairs to give us a little more room. "Such as?"

"You returning to work."

Upton's shoulders went back, and a bite of uncertainty dulled his eyes. "I'm not sure."

"Well, I am," Ryker returned. "You're ready."

His eyes sought Sebastian's, and when he nodded in encouragement, Upton's gaze traveled around the rest of the group. Each one of them smiled and concurred with Ryker, who appeared to be the one in charge, despite the equal shares they all held in the business.

Eventually, he turned to me. No idea why. This wasn't a decision I had any business poking my nose into. But when he looked at me, and I read his eyes, pleading with me to give my opinion, I relented.

"I think it's exactly what you need. It's the logical next step."

His tongue jutted into the inside of his cheek, and he suddenly found pushing his cuticle back with his thumbnail to be the most important thing he could do right now. And then his head came up and he clasped my hand under the table. "Okay."

All the guys rose from their chairs and gathered around him. There were hugs and slapping of backs in that way guys always did. I caught Athena's eye across the table. She smiled and nodded in approval.

I hadn't underestimated how hard it must have been for this close-knit group to lose one of their own. Upton didn't die in that bomb, but the way he cut himself off from those who loved and adored him, he might as well have. But watching them now, the happiness shining in their eyes, a surge of pride filled my chest. I'd helped get him to this point, and not because we'd ended up in bed together. Upton had walked a long way down the road to recovery before we'd even kissed—even if he hadn't been aware at the time—because he had, in fact, been ready. All he'd needed was a nudge in the right direction. A nudge I'd given him.

Zak wheeled himself around the table and came to sit beside me. "Well done, sis," he murmured. "On both counts."

I frowned. "What do you mean, both counts?"

"For helping a guy who desperately needed someone like you," he said. "And for landing a billionaire." He accompanied the latter with a twinkle in his eye and an overexaggerated wink.

"Jerk," I stated, my favorite insult when it came to my brother. I leaned closer. I didn't want Upton to hear this. "Do you think Marin would forgive me?"

An odd expression, kind of like a flash of anger, crossed my brother's face, but it disappeared so fast, I questioned whether it had been there at all.

"There's nothing to forgive," Zak said, a tic quivering in his cheek. "You're not doing anything wrong. Marin isn't here, and Upton is. You're entitled to live your life, sis. You've suffered enough."

"I'm not sure that's true," I said, although my response was tinged with a hint of irony. The crushing guilt I'd lived with for the past year and a half certainly felt lighter these last few weeks. The lump of steel that had sat on my chest ever since I'd gotten news of the bomb wasn't there anymore. I wouldn't say the pain had completely gone, and I didn't know if it ever would, but it had eased. Considerably.

"Oh, believe me," Zak replied with an edge to his tone, one I couldn't place. "It's true."

"What's going on?" I said, the invisible twin connection firing like crazy. "What are you not telling me?"

"Nothing," he said, seeming far too shifty for my liking. "But you're twenty-three, Belle. You have your whole life ahead of you. I never once blamed you for what happened, but that didn't mean I escaped the pain of knowing that *you did.* It killed me every time I'd see guilt sweep across your face when you looked at me, or a TV program came on that you used to watch with Marin, or some news anchor dug up footage of that night for some ungodly reason. Your heart has always been filled with kindness, and the decision you made that day to help the old lady rather than go to a concert with your fiancé, one that he'd eagerly anticipated for months, shows even more how selfless you are. You knew Marin would be disappointed you chose your job over him, yet you did it anyway because, deep down, you believed it was the right thing to do."

I rested my head on his shoulder. "Love you, bro."

"Not as much as I love you."

"Hey, are you pinching my girl?" Upton interjected.

I grinned. "Well, since you were getting so many hugs, I thought I'd grab one of my own with my twin."

"You're twins?" Athena asked. "Oh, I always wanted to be a twin."

"And instead, you got Elliot," Ryker drawled.

She smiled, but it didn't quite reach her eyes. I guessed she was as worried about her brother as the rest of them, probably more so. She rubbed her swollen stomach, and as if an unspoken conversation happened between them, Ryker put his hand over hers, his eyes seeming to convey a silent message.

"We should get back," Ryker said. "I'm sure the last thing anyone here wants is for Athena to go into labor in Upton's backyard."

"No offense, Athena, but yeah, that is the last thing I want," Garen offered, earning a dig in the ribs from Catriona. He didn't appear in the least bit troubled at her obvious reproach. That one must be a hell of a handful, although from the little I'd witnessed, Catriona could handle him just fine.

"Upton, call me tomorrow and we'll discuss a phased return to work," Ryker said, his tone brooking no argument.

There would be no backtracking for Upton, not that I expected him to, but Ryker clearly wanted to ensure his message was received loud and clear, and give very little wriggle room for Upton to change his mind.

"Sure," Upton said. "I'll see you guys out."

"We should make a move, too," Garen said. "Catriona and I have plans for this evening."

"We do?" she asked, surprised.

Garen pinched her hip. "Yeah, we do."

"Oh." She giggled and snuggled into his side.

"And us," Oliver said. "The kids have school tomorrow."

"That just leaves me then," Sebastian said. "Think I might hang around for a couple days if that's okay with you guys."

"Works for me," Upton said, although he narrowed his eyes at Sebastian as if he read something else into his desire to stay in LA rather than return to London.

"Come on, Zak," I said. "Let's get you home."

"You're coming back, yeah?" Upton asked, the pleading in his tone bringing a smile to my face.

"Tomorrow," I replied, flicking my eyes in Sebastian's direction. "I'm sure you two have a bit of catching up to do."

"Yeah," Sebastian said. "I need to kick his ass at Fortnite."

"Dream on," Upton scoffed.

He and Sebastian stood by the door waving us off as I

followed several cars winding their way down his driveway. As soon as we steered onto the main road, Zak shifted his focus to me.

"So, do you get to keep the car, now?"

I shook my head. "You really are a class-A jerk, you know that?"

Zak laughed. "I do have a bit of news if you're interested. Although since you seem to think I'm an idiot and all..."

He trailed off, knowing he'd piqued my curiosity enough for me to cave in. "Fine, what news?"

"I got to talking to Oliver and Elliot last night, and they want me to work with them."

I shot him a quick glance to check if he was teasing me, then returned my attention to the road. Up here in the mountains, the roads were pretty unforgiving. "Doing what?"

"They're looking to drive more diversity across the varying businesses under the ROGUES brand and they want me to be an ambassador, to help shape the specific needs of people with disabilities and ensure they have access to the best accessible technology."

"Oh, Zak." Tears sprang to my eyes. Zak's accident hadn't stopped his ambition or his drive, but we lived in a world where, sadly, sometimes disabilities made it harder to succeed. It wasn't right, but that didn't make its existence any less real. "That's such a fantastic opportunity."

"Yeah, it is."

I risked another look and, as I took in the pride in his expression, I reached for his hand and squeezed it. "They're lucky to have you."

22

Upton

"Walk me to the door," I said as I clasped Belle's hand.

She tipped back her head and squinted in the bright sunshine. "Nervous?"

"A little," I admitted.

Today was my first day back at work. True to his promise, Ryker had pushed hard for me to return almost immediately. I'd held him off for a week, but in the end, I'd capitulated to his demands. Strange how quickly you lost confidence when out of the game for a while, and given almost seventeen months had passed since I'd last entered this building as 'The Boss', my confidence sat at an all-time low.

See, the problem with being the person at the top of the tree was that everyone expected you to have all the answers, to stride about with self-assurance and poise, to lead from the front. I barely remembered how to put on a tie this morning, let alone head up a board of smart go-getters who'd look to me for guidance, direction, and leadership.

Antonio had agreed to stay on for a week to give me at least the beginnings of a handover, but given his tenure at the helm had lasted a lot longer than anyone had anticipated—apart from me—he had other responsibilities vying for his attention. He'd done ROGUES a favor by stepping in, but Antonio ran his own very successful company, and he needed to get back to it. How he'd managed to juggle the two for this long was testament to the man's talent.

"It'll be fine, you know," Belle said as she leaned her head on my shoulder. "In a few hours it'll feel as if you've never been away."

We reached the front entrance of my building, and I drew to a halt. "Maybe. Listen, I've been thinking."

"Ooh, that's dangerous." Her eyes twinkled with mirth.

"Ha ha. Very funny. Anyway, it's about your contract."

She stiffened, and her eyes filled with apprehension. "What about it?"

"Well," I began. "The contract was to act as a companion to me, and encourage me back into the land of the living, correct?"

She hesitated, and her eyes flitted about. "Yes."

"And… here I am. Task complete."

Her eyes went so wide, the whites were visible the entire way around her striking green irises. "So, you're saying I'm, what, fired?"

"Precisely," I said.

Her jaw slackened, and then her eyes hardened. "Wonderful. Have a nice life. Hope you'll be very happy."

She spun around to march away, but I caught her wrist before she got very far. "Hold up, gorgeous."

"Why should I?" she snapped. "I'm fired, you just told me that, so I can go where I damn well please. And don't call me gorgeous."

A laugh burst out of me. "Why not? You are. Gorgeous, that is."

It took her a while to catch on, but eventually, her expression filled with questions instead of ire.

"What are you playing at, Upton Barrick?" she asked.

"Ooh, you're full-naming me. I must be in trouble." I fake shuddered. "I kinda like being the subject of your rage. It turns me on."

She pulled out of my grip and folded her arms. "You have two seconds to tell me what's going on, or I'll-I'll—"

I snagged her around the waist and pulled her flush to my body, uncaring of the throngs of people hurrying by on their way to work.

"You'll what? What will you do, Belle?"

"Argh." She slammed her palm into my shoulder. "Stop playing games, you annoying man."

I bent my head and took her mouth, thoroughly kissing her right here in the middle of downtown LA. She melted against me, her body folding into mine. By the time I withdrew, her eyes were hazy and her lips swollen. She'd never looked more beautiful.

"I don't need a companion, but I do need a girlfriend. I need you. By my side, holding me up when I stumble, acting as a sounding board when I need direct, unfiltered feedback. I need you in my life, my bed. My house." I caught her hips and tugged her closer. "Move in with me."

"Whoa." Her hands came up. "Move in? With you?"

Sensing her shock, I backtracked. "When you're ready, yes. It doesn't have to be now. I know this is all very sudden, but I wanted to let you know my intentions. I realize you have Zak and your mom to consider, but I can help with that, too. We can move them closer to us. A purpose-built house fit for Zak's wheelchair, maybe, or one that we can adapt. A place he can be truly independent."

Truth be told, she appeared hellishly stunned. I guess this had come a little out of the blue, although it had been on my mind since we first slept together the night of my birthday party. We'd just *fit,* y'know? In every way. Physically, emotionally, sexually. I'd had enough sexual encounters over the years to know the difference between a passing fancy and a woman who might, just might, be the real deal. And I didn't plan on letting her go. Somehow I'd gotten lucky and stumbled upon the right woman for me.

"That's a lot to take in." She rubbed her forehead.

"Don't say anything now," I rushed to say in case she jumped to a decision. The wrong decision. "Mull it over, and we can talk more later. Let's have dinner together tonight."

"I still need to earn money, Upton. If I'm no longer working for you, then I'll have to start applying for jobs."

That soft groove appeared between her eyebrows. The one I always wanted to kiss. So I did. "We'll work it out."

Her lips thinned as she pressed them together. "I won't be kept, Upton. I'm not that kind of girl."

I chuckled. "Yeah, I figured that out a long time ago. Seriously, take the day. Go walk Bandit for me. I don't want him getting some kind of separation anxiety on his first day without me at the house. Then, tonight, we'll talk."

She nodded, sending a flush of relief rushing through me.

"Okay." She turned to walk away, then stopped. "What time do you want me to pick you up this evening?"

I'd asked Belle to drive me to the office. Before the accident, I had a driver, but I let him go. I really should think about rehiring him if he was still available, or if he wasn't, then consider interviewing for the position. I liked using the journey to and from the office as a way to catch up on emails I'd missed overnight or during the day. No doubt I'd return to that habit in a matter of days. It wouldn't take long to become entrenched in the day-to-day craziness of running a global organization.

"Around five-thirty?"

"I'll be here."

I watched her as she walked away, hips swaying. Great. Now I was hard. Fastening my jacket over the bulge in my trousers, I entered the building.

Gonna be a hell of a day.

Dropping my sunglasses in place, I scanned the street for Belle's car. My shoulders and back ached from sitting in a chair all day, something I hadn't done in so long that all my muscles had forgotten what it was like. I vowed that, tomorrow, I'd take regular breaks until I readjusted.

Belle had been right, though. By the time the second meeting ended, I'd settled into my groove, and when I hosted a working lunch with the mayor, it felt as if I'd never been away.

Her car drew to a halt, and the window went down. "Hey, handsome," she called out. "Need a ride?"

"Maybe," I said. "What's on offer?"

She dropped her gaze to my groin and, very purposefully, licked her lips. "That's negotiable."

I groaned and opened the car door, then jumped in. My mouth was on hers seconds later, and when our tongues touched, my dick hardened. I clasped her wrist and placed her hand over my erection. "Is this on the menu?"

"Oh, yeah." She squeezed. "That, and a lot more besides."

"Then drive, woman. I've had a long, hard day, and I know exactly what will relax me."

Laughing, she put the car in drive and, after checking over her shoulder, pulled into the traffic.

"So, how was it?" she asked.

"As if I'd never been away."

"Ha," she said. "Told you so."

"No one likes a clever dick." I couldn't stop my lips from curling at the edges.

She put her hand on my groin. “I do. I love a clever dick.”

I threw back my head and laughed. Damn, this woman. I fucking loved her.

Wait…

No I didn’t.

I didn’t love her.

Did I?

Fuck, how should I know. I’d never been in love.

I should ask one of the guys what it felt like. Not Garen, though. He’d probably say something along the lines of “When all you can think about is fucking her night and day”. Ryker wouldn’t be any use either. And as for Seb… if what he felt was love, then I wanted no part of it. The man was in purgatory. I’d rather take a pass.

One thing I did know: what I felt for Belle was different to the feelings I’d had for every other woman I’d ever dated. With them, it was all about sex. But with her… I liked everything. Sharing a coffee out on the patio. Taking Bandit for a walk. Watching some cheesy movie on Netflix. Sure, sex crossed my mind often. Like every five minutes, maybe. But it wasn’t the only thing I thought about. She shared my life, and I never wanted that to change.

“Have you thought any more about what I said this morning?”

“Duh,” she said, accompanying her response with a roll of her eyes. “I’ve thought about nothing else.”

“And?”

I held my breath, expecting rejection, hoping for assent.

“Moving in, Upton, it’s such a big step. We haven’t known each other all that long.”

“I know enough,” I said.

“Can I be honest?”

“When have you ever been anything else?”

She chuckled. “True. Look, here’s the thing.”

No. Not "The Thing". I hated "The Thing". It always means you won't like the next comment.

"You haven't engaged with the world around you for such a long time, and I'm worried that you're... on the rebound, maybe. I know that sounds crazy, but I'd feel a lot better if we had this conversation in a couple of weeks or a month. Let life in again and see what happens."

"I won't change my mind," I insisted.

"I hope you don't."

Optimism surged through my veins. That wasn't a straight-up no. I'd accept a 'wait and see'.

She sighed. "In the meantime, I need to find a job."

If it were up to me, I'd dump a whole load of cash in her bank account on a monthly basis and move her family into a house more suitable for Zak's disability than where they currently lived. But she'd fight me all the way on it, particularly the former, so instead, I said, "Would you at least allow me to make some calls? It's what every boyfriend would do for his girl."

She side-eyed me and gave me a soft smile. "That'd be great."

23

Belle

"Zak, pack it in. I'm going to be late."

Zak grinned and held the butter out of reach, swapping it from hand to hand every time I made a move to grasp it.

I lunged again. Missed. Again. "You are such an asshole."

"Zakhary Laker, give your sister the butter," Mom interjected as she entered the kitchen. "The first day at a new job is hard enough without you teasing her unnecessarily."

Zak reluctantly handed over the butter, and I stuck out my tongue. Childish, but that was the way Zak and I always rolled. We'd never really grown up when dealing with each other—and in a way, I prayed we never did.

"I hope those poor old dears know what they're in for," Zak said, swigging juice straight out of the carton and earning a glare from Mom for his troubles. "Imagine, you get to the ripe old age of eighty-something and then you realize your twilight years are going to be filled with Miss Bossy Boots taking care of you."

I shot a glance at Mom, then flipped Zak the bird.

He laughed. "You're lucky Mom's back is turned."

Mom glanced over her shoulder, but by then, I'd retracted said finger. I slathered butter and grape jelly over my toast and flopped into a chair at the kitchen table.

"I still don't understand why you've taken this job," Zak continued. "What's the point in having a boyfriend who could clear California's debt in one fell swoop, and choosing to slog your guts out at a retirement home ten hours a day."

"Because," I grabbed the juice before he drank the entire carton, "some of us have pride."

I hadn't told my family about Upton's bolt-out-of-the-blue offer to move in as well as buy a home for Mom and Zak. I wasn't sure what their response would be, and I needed to come to this decision on my own. I'd thought of nothing else for the past four weeks, though, but to be fair to Upton, he hadn't brought up the subject once, leaving me to mull it over in my own time.

The question that lurked at the back of my mind, the one that prevented me from diving headlong into a future with him, was whether he felt some kind of gratitude toward me for leading him back into the world, and that was clouding his judgement. He hadn't told me he loved me, nor had I said those words back to him, and until we faced up to our true feelings and genuinely put our pasts behind us, the idea of a permanent move was out of the question.

I did love him. At least I thought so, but everything had happened so fast, and I needed time to catch my breath. And so did Upton, no matter what he thought to the contrary.

"Pride comes before a fall that breaks your pretty little nose, sis," Zak said.

"I'll break your nose if you don't shut up," I muttered.

"Like to see you try," Zak hit back.

"Oh, for goodness' sake, will you two give it a rest? Please."

Mom dug her fingertips into her temples. "Five minutes of peace in the mornings. That's all I ask."

I frowned. "Mom, are you okay?"

Mom hardly ever lost her temper. My friends at school used to be terribly jealous of her serene attitude to everything. She glided through life letting very little bother her. Considering she'd worked multiple jobs since our deadbeat father had walked out on her when we were babies, it was a testament to how lucky we were to have her as our mom.

"Yes, yes, it's fine." She motioned through the air with her hand. "An unexpected bill arrived in the mail yesterday, that's all." She smiled, but it didn't hold. "Nothing to worry about."

"Ask Belle's rich boyfriend to pay," Zak said, unashamed.

"Jesus, Zak." I glared at him, while Mom clipped him around the ear.

"We pay our way, Zakhary Laker," Mom said, full-naming him for the second time this morning.

"I have some savings, Mom," I said. "Even though Upton fired me as his companion, Sebastian paid me the completion bonus anyway. Said I'd earned it." I laughed. "He wasn't wrong. Anyway, whatever you need, it's yours."

I'd have to put off buying my own car until I'd saved up again, but as Upton hadn't mentioned taking back the car he'd loaned me, I hoped he might let me keep it for a little while longer.

Mom patted the back of my hand. "Thank you, sweetheart."

I noticed she didn't decline the offer which meant she truly needed the money.

God, maybe I should take Upton up on his invite to move in. That way, the pressure would reduce on Mom, too.

No, I couldn't. She'd instilled morals and values in me, buried them so deep, there was no way of digging them out. We were a proud family. Even Zak's suggestions were tongue-in-cheek. Not for one second did he expect me to ask Upton for money to help us out.

"Right, gotta go. Wish me luck."

"Break a leg, sis," Zak said. "Well, not actually, but you know what I mean."

Mom walked me to the door, but her hand on my arm stopped me from opening it. "I hate taking your money, Belle, and I promise I'll pay every cent back."

"Mom, don't be silly. You've done everything for me and Zak. You don't owe me anything." I frowned. "What was the bill for?"

She grimaced. "Zak. Seems the hospital keep finding new charges that I haven't settled."

I wrapped my arms around her and gave her a hug. "Mom, we're not children any longer, and you don't need to keep things like this from us. We're a family, and families stick together."

She palmed my cheek. "You're such a good girl, Belle."

"And you're the best mom a girl could ever have."

I grabbed my purse from my room and slung it over my shoulder. "Right, I'd better go. Don't want to be late on my first day."

I stepped outside—and shock hit me squarely in the chest.

Where the hell is Upton's car?

The space where I'd parked it on the street last night lay empty. Oh Christ, some little bastard must have stolen it. I pinched the bridge of my nose. How on earth would I tell him his car had been stolen? And as if that wasn't bad enough, now I'd be late for my first day at my new job.

What a brilliant way to make a first impression—not.

I dug my phone out of my bag to call the police when a high-pitched whistle startled me. I glanced in the direction of the noise.

"Lose something?"

My jaw dropped. Upton was a little way down the street holding the biggest bunch of flowers I'd ever seen, and next to him, wrapped in a big red bow, was a brand-new SUV in candy-apple red—my favorite color.

"What's going on?" I asked, making my way over to him.

He twisted his lips to one side in a wry smile. "I'm afraid that since you're no longer my employee, I've had to confiscate the company vehicle. However," he added, "I thought this might compensate."

He thrust the flowers at me with one hand and held up a car key with the other. I, on the other hand, stood with my knees locked in place and my mouth flapping like a poor fish tossed onto the quayside.

"It's German. The most reliable of all vehicles, in my opinion. If you really don't like it, though, we can return it and swap it for one you do like."

"It's... it's a car."

Upton grinned. "There's no fooling you, is there?"

"You can't buy me a car."

"Erm, I think you'll find I can do whatever I damn well please. I'm a rebel like that."

"But—"

"No buts. It's yours. And please, please don't utter a single word about charity or favors or shit like that. You are my girlfriend. Today is your first day in a new job, and I, as the man in your life, wanted to buy you a little gift to mark a special day."

"A little gift? Jesus, Upton, a box of candy is a little gift." I shook my head. "You've done so much for me already."

"No, Belle." He removed the flowers from my arms and set them on the passenger seat of the car, then slipped his arms around my waist and pulled me close. "It's you who's done so much for me. If it weren't for your dogged determination to show me that I had a life worth living, then I'd still be hiding away in my too-big house, swamped with guilt I didn't know how to deal with."

He bent his head and kissed me, right there on the street outside Mr. Clifford's house. I'd bet the old man had his nose pressed up against the pane of glass in his living room and was right this second on the verge of calling the police and reporting us for lewd conduct.

Screw him. I didn't care.

I wrapped my arms around his neck and buried my fingers in his soft hair. Right here, with this man who a few short months ago I'd never met, was my happy place.

He drew back, pecked my lips a couple times, then grinned. "You'd better get a move on, or you'll be late."

He removed the bow and folded it up, then opened the car door, and I got in. The smell of leather and newness hit me, and I placed my hands on the steering wheel, stunned that this beautiful car was mine.

"Oh, before I forget to mention," Upton said, "there's a fully functioning wheelchair lift in the back, so Zak won't have any trouble getting in and out."

Tears rushed to my eyes. No one had ever done anything like this for me before.

"Thank you," I whispered.

"No, thank you. See you tonight. Good luck, not that you'll need it." He bent his head, gave me a final kiss, and then he was gone.

On the entire journey to my new place of work, I kept getting hit with moments of disbelief. Upton had bought me a car. *A car.* And he'd even thought about Zak with the lift.

How did I get so lucky?

The day I saw the advert for a companion had changed my life. It had been tough in the beginning, but these last few weeks, everything had fallen into place. Only one question remained outstanding, and despite Upton's generosity this morning, I still didn't have an answer for him. In a way, his gift made it harder to take that final step, as if by agreeing to move in after such an expensive present, it would send a message that his money had enticed me when the truth was that his money made this a far more difficult decision to reach.

I arrived at the retirement home to find the manager waiting for me. A middle-aged lady with graying hair that she wore in a fashionable bob that reached her shoulders, Mrs. Compton exuded a warm and caring spirit. When I'd come for my interview, we'd hit it off immediately. Twin Palms nursing home was one of the best in the state with a waiting list a mile long, and the desire to work here was equally sought after. To land an assistant manager job had been something of a coup for me, and even though Upton had carved out the introduction, he'd sworn on his life that he hadn't exerted any influence in the final decision. Mrs. Compton was a woman who knew her own mind. I couldn't see her allowing anyone to pen her into a corner or force her into a decision she didn't want to make.

"Belle, you're right on time." She extended her hand, and I shook it. "Come on in. Our residents are all anxious to meet you."

The morning passed in a blur of introductions and procedures, and by the time it reached one o'clock, I was more than ready for a break and a chance to reflect on the day so far. Mom had packed a sandwich and an apple for me, and as the weather was so nice today, I took them out into the gardens to eat.

I sat on a bench facing a row of soft pink rosebushes and turned my face up to the sun. My shoulders relaxed, and a sense of peace came over me. Already, after a few short hours, I knew I'd made the right decision to come and work here. The residents were all so lovely, and the other staff had welcomed me so warmly, I already felt as if I belonged. I couldn't wait to tell Upton all about it over dinner tonight.

"Hello, Belle."

My eyes snapped open, and I sat up straight, squinting into the bright sunshine in time to see Marin's brother, Wyatt, take a seat beside me. A prickle of unease settled at the base of my spine. When Zak told me he was relocating to Florida, it'd been the best news I could have received. We'd never exactly hit it off, and after Marin died, Wyatt had laid the blame squarely at my feet. At the time he'd said some pretty nasty things, each one uncalled for because no one could have made me feel any worse than I already did.

"Wyatt, what are you doing here? I thought you'd moved to the East Coast?"

"I have."

He reached into my sandwich box and helped himself to half my lunch. I almost snatched it back but decided it wasn't worth the effort.

"How did you find me here?" I asked with a frown. "It's my first day today."

He bit into the sandwich and chewed, then swallowed. "I stopped by your house this morning. I'm only back for a few days. Got a couple of bits and pieces to tie up, and I had an idea you might want to visit Marin's grave with me. I don't know when I'll be back again."

Although going anywhere with him, including Marin's grave, was right at the top of my list of 'not this side of hell freezing over', news of his impending departure and unlikely return filled me with relief. I could do this one thing and then never see him again.

"Oh. Sure. I don't finish my shift until five, but we can go after that if you like." I'd text Upton to tell him I'd be an hour or so late. "I presume Zak told you where I'd be."

"No. I never got as far as your front door."

"Then how did you... oh."

"Yeah, oh." He snorted, and when he set his eyes on me, they were filled with hatred. "Nice show you put on, by the way. It didn't make me sick to my stomach at all to see my brother's fiancée with her tongue down another guy's throat."

"Wyatt," I began, but he cut me off with a hand slice through the air.

"Bagged yourself a rich dude, huh, Belle? Marin a long-forgotten memory?"

"No!" I expelled.

"Bullshit. My brother's body is still warm in his grave, yet you've already moved on. Nice car, by the way. Was that in payment for a blow job, perhaps?"

I struck him across the face, only the sting in my palm and the handprint on Wyatt's cheek letting me know I'd hit him at all.

"Fuck you," I spat out, anger and indignation sending me to my feet. "You don't know anything about me. Anything at all."

"I know my brother fucking loved you."

"And I loved him."

He snorted. "Sure you did."

"I did! But he's dead, Wyatt. I can't change that."

He raked me with a disdainful gaze. "Yeah, we all know your culpability when it comes to my brother."

I doubled over, air forcibly ejected from my lungs by Wyatt's cruel yet truthful words. My stomach dropped to the grass-covered ground at my feet, and I heaved a couple of times as nausea filled my stomach. "I know what I did," I whispered. "And I've paid for it over and over."

"You haven't paid nearly enough," Wyatt spat. "Sixteen months. That's all it's been. Sixteen fucking months. Was my brother so easy to forget that you feel zero remorse for warming another man's bed?"

I tried to defend myself, but the words wouldn't come. Maybe Wyatt had a point, one I needed to examine a little closer. Was this why I'd avoided answering Upton's question about moving in, because I still wasn't over Marin? Or did I just feel guilty that I'd found love again? Was I on the rebound and what I felt for Upton wasn't real after all?

Questions, questions, questions. My head spun with the number racing through my mind. And all the while, Wyatt sat there, relishing in my pain.

"You never liked me, did you?" I'd never asked him this, but there'd always been an undercurrent between us, and my intuition had picked up on his antipathy. I remember asking Marin about it once, and he'd replied with, "Wyatt hates everyone. Himself most of all." I hadn't asked him to expand at the time. Now I wish I had.

"That's not what this is about, but if you must know, no, I didn't. My brother deserved better, and damn if you haven't proved me right."

Hot tears pricked my eyes, the second time today that I'd almost cried except, on this occasion, the tears were brought about by hurt and anger, both at Wyatt and myself.

"I have to get back," I said, picking up the remains of my lunch. I hadn't touched a bite. "I'm sorry, Wyatt. Have a safe trip back to Florida."

"You should be sorry," he called at my retreating back. "Once a bitch, always a bitch."

His words stung, but I kept my shoulders back, my head held high, and returned to work.

Whatever Wyatt hoped to achieve by coming here today, he'd succeeded in one thing.

He'd put doubt in my mind.

24

Upton

I twirled a lock of Belle's hair around my forefinger, my attention more on her than the show she'd chosen on Netflix. Ever since she'd arrived this evening, she'd been quiet, but despite several tender probing questions from me, she'd insisted there was nothing wrong and put her taciturn responses down to exhaustion after her first day at a new job.

I didn't buy it. She'd been so excited this morning when I'd dropped off her new car. I'd taken a risk gifting it to her. Belle was a proud woman who didn't take kindly to anything she saw as charity, but I'd wanted to do something nice, and when she'd accepted almost without a murmur, I'd driven the entire journey to work with a stupid grin on my face. Even during several grueling and tricky meetings today, my smile had barely dropped.

Yet over the past three hours I'd hardly managed to coax a full sentence out of her, and the newness of our relationship meant I'd jumped to the worst possible conclusion.

I was losing her.

When she let out a heavy sigh, I reached for the remote control and turned the TV off. She glanced up at me, surprise raising her eyebrows.

"Bored with the show?"

"No. I am, however, irked at the fact you refuse to tell me what's wrong."

She struggled to sit up, shuffling a little distance away from me. "I told you. Nothing's wrong. I'm tired, that's all. Mrs. Compton hit me with a ton of information today, and I'm trying to process it all."

Belle was just about the worst liar I'd ever seen. Her eyes got all shifty, and she would pluck at invisible fluff on whatever she happened to be wearing, just like she was doing now. But I knew her well enough by now to know that the more I pushed, the less she'd talk. I'd have to play the long game. The problem with that was I'd never been the most patient of men. In business, I pressed, coerced, used knowledge and research to force my opponent to concede.

Except, Belle wasn't an opponent—and we weren't in a boardroom.

I got to my feet and extended my hand in her direction. "Let's take Bandit for a walk on the beach."

She frowned. "It's dark out."

"So. I'll take a flashlight, and there are streetlights anyway. Besides, this way, we'll have the beach to ourselves."

"Okay." She rose from the couch. "You fetch Bandit, and I'll go get my jacket."

We reconvened in the hallway. Bandit couldn't wait to get outside, pushing his nose in the gap before I'd properly opened the door. He leaped over the step, going to the very limits of his extendable lead and, despite his size, he almost yanked my arm out of my socket, then glanced back as if to say, "Hurry up".

Damned dog.

I closed the door and linked my fingers with Belle's, half expecting her to pull away. Relief that she didn't surged through me. I felt as if I was clinging to the cliff edge with the sodden earth crumbling all around me. You'd think with my history, I'd be used to how life could turn on a dime. One minute, everything was perfect. Well, maybe not perfect, but better than most. The next, bam! It all came crashing down, that solid foundation you'd built, and you realized you had very little control over your own destiny.

We walked in silence, Bandit's panting the only noise filling the night air. Twenty minutes after leaving the house, we jogged down the narrow stone steps that led to the beach. I flicked on the flashlight which lit our path and bent down to unclip Bandit's lead. He immediately sped off, a pale blur in the inky darkness.

"What if we lose him?" Belle asked, her tone filled with concern.

I whistled, and seconds later, he slid to a halt at my feet and sat, waiting for the treat he knew was coming, then ran off again, his joy at simply running free seeping into my bones and giving me a sense of optimism. Maybe Belle was telling the truth: she'd had a hard day with a lot of new information tossed at her, and her quiet reflection was how she processed it before a new day arrived. I should give her the benefit of the doubt. If there was something wrong, she'd tell me in her own time and her own way.

"His recall really is fantastic," she said, leaning her head on my shoulder as we padded through the soft golden sand, cool now that the sun had set. "You should be proud of the work you've done with him."

"I can't imagine not having him now," I admitted. "Although the little shit drives me crazy at least ten times a day."

She tipped back her head and peered up at me. "That's dogs for you. They're like kids. You're glad you have them, but damn if some days you don't want them to just leave you the hell alone."

I chuckled, comforted that she'd shared more than a couple of words with me. That entire sentence was more than I'd gotten out of her all evening.

"Do you want kids?" I asked.

I'd anticipated the question would bring her closer to me. Instead, she slipped her hand from mine and put a good foot between us. "One day. Maybe."

A spike of anxiety shot up my spine. Not because she'd sounded uncommitted about kids. Hell, she was only twenty-three, and my question had been conversational rather than a deep and meaningful discussion about the merits, or otherwise, of leaving behind something of yourself. No, that tingle that reminded me of a static electric shock had more to do with how fast she'd disengaged.

I stopped walking. Belle carried on, her concentration fixed on the sand beneath her feet. It took her a second or two to realize I wasn't beside her. She pulled up and slowly turned around.

"What's the matter?"

"Good question," I said as my arms came across my chest.

She frowned. "I'm confused."

"That makes two of us." Two steps brought me face to face with her.

She huffed. "Why are you talking in riddles?"

"Talk to me, Belle," I pleaded. "Something isn't right, and I'm just not buying the whole 'I'm tired' excuse. You've been distant all night. I want to know what's wrong. How can I help you if you won't tell me what's going on in that head of yours?"

"Just leave it, please."

Her voice was so quiet, I had to strain to hear her despite the absence of a breeze and the only sound being the waves gently washing onto the shoreline.

I cupped her face, angling her head to give her no choice other than to meet my gaze. The moon reflected in her eyes, and she'd never looked more beautiful to me.

"I can't leave it. I—" I shook my head, the words "I love you" on the tip of my tongue. Something prevented me from saying them, though, an invisible barrier I couldn't break through. Maybe it was because I'd never told a woman I loved her that made the words stick in my throat. Or maybe I was scared she wouldn't say them back. "Never mind."

My arms fell to my sides, and I whistled for Bandit to return. He arrived in seconds, his pink tongue on full display, his eyes bright with excitement at the rare and unexpected treat of a run on the beach after dark. He plunked his rump on the ground and swiped at me with his paw.

"Here you go, boy."

He snaffled the treat and swallowed. I clipped his lead onto his collar and set off for home.

"Marin's brother, Wyatt, came to see me today."

I halted in my tracks and turned around to find Belle with her chin tucked into her chest, toeing the sand with her right foot.

"Oh?" I framed it as a question, determined that now that she'd started the conversation, I'd let her go at her own pace. Already, I sensed that the visit from her dead fiancé's brother wasn't a welcome one. If she'd greeted his return favorably, she'd have told me about him earlier.

"He called by the house this morning."

"This morning?" I frowned. If she spoke with him before she left the house, then he wasn't the cause of her distance this evening. Which beggared the question: what was? "Before I got there?"

"I don't know."

I shook my head as though that would empty the confused

thoughts from my mind. I held back the temptation to hit her with a barrage of questions as I would if this was a work situation. Clearly she was struggling to articulate what had happened. The best way to handle this was to let her tell it in her own way.

"I went into the gardens at work today to eat my lunch, and he just appeared."

"But you said he came by the house?" I rubbed my forehead, even more bewildered. "I don't understand."

"He saw us. When you gave me the car, he was watching."

Watching? Like some fucking creeper?

Not feeling any better about Wyatt.

"And he waited to catch you at lunch? For what purpose?"

Her eyes filled up, and she blinked rapidly to clear the approaching tears.

What the ever-loving fuck?

"Belle." I cradled her face, my thumbs brushing her cheeks. "What did he say?"

I tried—and failed—to keep the note of steel out of my voice. If this bastard had upset her in some way, I'd rip off his arms.

She nibbled her bottom lip and shook her head.

Fury bolted through my veins, and I had to take a huge breath, and hold it down in my lungs for a few seconds as a way to stop myself bellowing "Tell me right now!" I didn't know this guy, but already my intuition had shot straight to Defcon Five. She looked… broken.

"He gave me a lot to think about, that's all."

"Such as?"

Bandit tugged on his lead, anxious to set off now that I'd tethered him. I tugged back, and he sat, peering up at me with his big brown eyes.

"It's only been a little over sixteen months," she whispered. "And here I am, with you, and it just… it just doesn't feel long enough. Like I haven't grieved enough. That I'm being disrespectful to Marin's memory."

Wyatt is a dead man.

"There isn't a manual to grief, Belle. No one can, or should, tell you how to grieve. We all cope with loss in different ways. Take me for example. I withdrew from the world. You carried on, taking care of Zak, of your mom. Neither of those approaches are wrong. They are personal, to us, to how we choose to deal with what we've lost."

I had the feeling every word I spoke was falling on deaf ears, and God, it scared me. It scared me more than I had been since that night. The night I lost Jenna. I'd felt her slipping away, and I had exactly the same sensation now, standing here on a darkened beach, in front of the woman I loved, desperately clinging on to her as she slipped away, too. Not in the same way my sister had, but just as finite all the same.

"We jumped into this too fast," she said, as if I hadn't spoken.

Her eyes were glazed. She'd withdrawn into herself, talking on autopilot without really being present.

"How can I trust my feelings for you when I'm still grieving? What if I'm on the rebound? How is that fair to you, especially after all you've gone through?"

"No way." I gripped her upper arms and shook her gently. "You're not on the rebound. I'd know. Fuck's sake, Belle. When I'm inside you, and you're looking at me, it's real. It's fucking real."

"How do you know?"

"Because I love you!" I yelled. "Jesus Christ, I love you. And that's real. It's real in here." I slammed my palm against my chest.

The amount of cursing was in direct response to the frustration surging inside me, like a tsunami whose progress I couldn't halt. Desperate men did desperate things, and as Belle slithered through my fingers, I blurted out the very thing that shouldn't be shared in a blaze of exasperation and anger. I wasn't angry at her. My rage was directed at Wyatt.

The way she staggered back a couple of feet, a stunned expression exploding on her face, meant those words had gotten through the barriers she'd erected, intended to keep me at bay. Just as I hoped they'd crash to the ground, she dashed my hopes with her next comments.

"You can't say that for sure. You've lived as a recluse for so long, Upton. How do you know that what you feel for me isn't gratitude that I helped you move on with your life?"

"You think I feel *gratitude?* You're the first thing I think of when I open my eyes each morning and the last thing I see when I close them at night, and you think that's because of *gratitude?* Do you really think I'm that shallow?"

"That's just it," she whispered. "I'm not sure we know each other enough for me to answer that question truthfully."

The knife, so perfectly aimed, sliced straight through my heart. I clutched my stomach and swallowed hard, feeling the color drain from my face. Everything inside me that Belle had painstakingly filled up with her patience and kindness bled out, swallowed up by the billions of grains of sand at my feet.

"Are you breaking up with me?"

She lowered her head, and her chin wobbled. "I don't want to."

A spark of hope restarted my heart with a jolt. "Then don't."

"But I can't commit like you want me to."

"If this is about moving in, forget it. We can take it slow. Whatever you want." I realized I'd succumbed to begging, but I didn't care. I'd do whatever it took for Belle not to crush me by walking away. Fuck pretending to be manly and an alpha-hole. All that mattered was that I didn't lose the woman standing in front of me.

She shook her head. "It's not just that. It's... oh God, I don't know. It's everything. I feel as if I'm betraying everything Marin and I stood for. We were getting *married.* If the security services had managed to stop that terrorist, I would be married right now. And yet less than seventeen months later, with my fiancé barely cold in the ground, I'm already warming your bed. What does that say about me?"

"That you're allowed a life of your own," I said as gently as I could manage. Yelling at her wouldn't work, although holding back on the impulse to shake her until her teeth rattled almost killed me. "That as much as you loved him..." I winced, then plowed on. "He's gone. And I'm here." I gathered her into my arms, hoping the physical connection would stitch us back together. She allowed me to kiss her, but when I tasted her tears, I withdrew.

Our eyes locked—and I instantly knew my worst fears had materialized.

I'd lost her.

"I think we both need some time apart," she said, averting her gaze. "I'm so sorry, Upton. I'll return the car, of course."

"Keep it," I spat bitterly. "It's worthless to me."

In my hurt and anger, I almost added "Just like you", except those weren't the three words I wanted to leave her with.

They were a lie.

25

Belle

"Belle, get up."

I rolled over in bed and faced the wall, giving Zak my back. "Go away."

Five days had passed since I had walked out on Upton after telling him we needed some time apart. And every single day since a lump of concrete had sat in my stomach, one that screamed "You've made a huge mistake". Not that concrete could talk, but you know what I mean. I felt sick, had hardly eaten, and I swore that my hair was falling out. A bit dramatic, maybe, but when I brushed it yesterday, I was sure there were more hairs entangled in the brush than on a normal day. The only thing I had managed to do was haul my ass out of bed each day to go to work. I put on a brave, smiling face for the residents, but the second I walked out the front door, my smile fell, and guess who arrived?

My new best friend—depression.

Wyatt's blunt assessment of what he saw as a betrayal of his brother's memory still rang in my ears. On reflection, sixteen months wasn't long to grieve over someone you'd planned to spend the rest of your life with. At the back of my mind I recalled reading something about Queen Victoria of England who mourned Prince Albert's passing for something like forty years, and here I was, jumping into bed with the first guy who showed me a little craved-for affection less than a year and a half later.

Except, deep in my heart, I knew Upton meant more to me than that. I kept thinking back to his comment about no one having a right to tell another how to grieve. That we each traveled that path alone.

Oh God, I'm so confused.

The competing—and opposite—desires made me feel as if I was on a boat in the middle of a horrendous storm. One minute I was pitched one way, and a second later, the other. I didn't know what to do for the best. Whatever I chose, someone got hurt.

Zak had been on at me to tell him what happened ever since I returned home on Monday night and broke the news that Upton and I had split. I hadn't mentioned Wyatt, or the cruel things he'd said to me. Zak would have shot straight into protective brother mode and wanted to fix things. Except he couldn't fix this. Somehow, I had to unearth the answers on my own.

His hot stare locked on to the back of my head—call it a twin thing that I knew that when I couldn't see him—and all I could hear was his steady breathing. Zak in this mood wasn't going anywhere until I faced up to his questions.

With a heavy sigh, I turned over, burrowing my hands beneath my pillow. "What?"

"Talk to me, sis. Tell me what's going on. This isn't like you."

"What isn't like me? Having a lie-in on Saturday morning

after working my ass off at a brand-new job? My brain is fried, Zak. I just need some space."

He snorted. "We shared a womb, Belle, and countless secrets since. I can tell when you're layering on the bullshit." He sniffed the air. "Can smell it, too."

Despite the resident gloom sitting on my shoulders, my lips twitched, but the smile didn't last. The longing to talk my problems through with the one person who knew me most in this entire world overcame me, and I blurted, "Wyatt came to see me."

Zak's eyebrows shot up in twin arcs. "Wyatt? When? Where?"

"Monday, at work. He accosted me in the gardens as I was having lunch."

"What the fuck did that tool want?"

Zak hadn't exactly buddied up with Marin as I'd hoped, but he liked him well enough. Unlike Wyatt. Another twin thing we had in common. We both intensely disliked Marin's older brother.

"Oh, you know, to offer me the benefit of his huge experience with relationships. And to call me a bitch and tell me I hadn't grieved long enough for his brother before jumping into bed with another man."

The incredulity followed by blind rage that crossed Zak's face made me glad I hadn't told him the part where Wyatt insinuated Upton had gifted me a car in return for sexual favors.

"He fucking what!" Zak roared, his voice carrying into the rest of the house.

Seconds later, before I'd had a chance to respond, Mom's head appeared around the door.

"What is all this noise? Zakhary? Izabelle?"

Whenever Mom full-named us, it meant we'd pissed her off. Neither of us spoke, and she shook her head.

"I am on the phone." She waved her cell in the air in case we misunderstood the meaning of the word *phone*. "Please keep it down."

She disappeared again, leaving me alone with Zak, and for my benefit, he reiterated his last comment, this time hissing it underneath his breath.

I fessed up. "Wyatt saw me with Upton. I didn't tell you because it seemed pointless, but when I left the house that morning, Upton was waiting for me with a huge bunch of flowers and a brand-new car."

"He bought you a car!" Zak said, then lowering his voice in case he received another dose of Mom's wrath, "a car?"

"Yes."

"I don't see a car sitting in the driveway," Zak helpfully pointed out.

I rolled my eyes at him. "I could hardly keep such an extravagant gift after we split up. I left it at his house on Monday night and caught the bus home. But that's not the point I'm trying to make. I kissed Upton that morning, and I guess Wyatt must have been watching."

"Fucking creep," Zak muttered, his face still red from my earlier revelation. And then his eyes widened. "Please tell me that useless piece of shit isn't the reason you split with the best thing that has ever happened to you."

I thought it interesting that he mustn't think that Marin was the best thing that had ever happened to me, but I decided not to tug on that particular thread right this minute.

"He gave me food for thought, that's all. He's right, Zak. Sixteen months isn't long. What if I'm on the rebound? What if Upton has latched on to the first woman he saw after emerging from a self-induced exile? What if the only thing we have in common is our dual loss and subsequent guilt? There are too many questions, and I'm not willing to make a huge mistake until I've answered them."

"What crap, Belle," Zak expelled. "I'm paralyzed, not blind. Anyone with half a brain can see how much you two are meant for one another."

I nibbled on my thumb, a shard of nail providing a welcome distraction. "Are we, though? Marin and I were perfect for each other, and look how that ended."

"Were you?" Zak asked.

"What does that mean?"

Zak hitched a shoulder. "Nothing. I'm just thinking out loud. Let me ask you this. Are you running from a relationship with Upton because you think you're on the rebound, or being disrespectful to Marin's memory? Or are you scared in case something awful happens to him and so you'd rather avoid the risk of falling in love with someone you might lose?"

I stared out the window and gave his questions due consideration. Zak remained quiet, allowing me some time to reflect. After almost a minute, I still didn't have an answer.

"I honestly don't know, Zak, which is precisely why I can't commit. I need to understand where my head's at before I can move forward."

"And Wyatt just threw in a hand grenade," Zak said, more to himself than to me.

I answered anyway. "He didn't help the situation, that's for sure."

Zak reversed his wheelchair and pointed it toward the door. "I'll leave you in peace. Next time, don't fucking shut me out."

I grinned. "I won't."

"Oh, and Belle, my advice for what it's worth? Don't take too long to make up your mind whether Upton is worth fighting for. A man like that won't hang around forever."

And with that bombshell, he left me alone with a jumble of thoughts and feelings I somehow had to make sense of.

One thing was certain: I couldn't afford to make a mistake.

For my sake—and Upton's.

26

Upton

When Zak and a guy I didn't recognize arrived unexpectedly at my house, my stomach flipped over. *God, please don't let anything have happened to Belle.*

I buzzed them in and went to wait by the front door. My palms were clammy, and adrenaline caused pins and needles in my hands and feet. As soon as the car stopped, I strode straight over to the passenger side.

"Is Belle okay?"

Zak nodded, and his unworried expression immediately allayed my fears. "She's fine. Sorry to barge in unannounced."

"You're welcome here anytime."

"This is Chad."

I nodded at his friend, then opened the trunk and took out Zak's wheelchair. Chad and I lifted it over the front step and then I led them through the house and outside to the patio.

"How's Belle doing?" I asked.

"Sad," Zak said. "She misses you."

I nodded, automatically seeking out the vast tree-lined garden as a way to anchor my emotions. "I miss her, too." I cut my gaze back to Zak's. "I still don't understand what went wrong."

"She's confused and scared, and stubborn as a fucking mule."

I chuckled. "I concur with the end of that statement."

"Listen," Zak said, leaning forward. "Don't let her walk away. Not like this. Push her, hard. You need to fight for her, force her to face up to the demons she's allowing to control her future, and help her shake them off."

I shook my head. "Sorry, Zak, but I can't do that. I won't coerce Belle into something she doesn't want. She made it clear on Monday that she needed time to work things through, and I respect her enough to give her that."

"Jesus," he groaned. "You're just as bad as she is."

My gaze fell to his hands where he'd clenched them into fists on top of the table. The right one was grazed. "What happened to you?"

He shot a glance at his friend then shrugged. "I went to see Wyatt. Marin's brother."

My jaw worked. "I know who he is," I ground out. "Belle told me he visited her at work. She didn't share what he said to her, but whatever it was, it made her doubt our relationship."

"Then you won't blame me for punching the sanctimonious bastard in the face."

My eyes widened, and then I grinned. "You hit him?" I clapped Zak on the shoulder. "Thanks. You saved me a job."

"He didn't just hit him," Chad interjected. "He knocked the fucker on his ass."

My smile grew. "Good."

"He got inside her head, Upton, and that's why she's at home right now instead of here with you. But she doesn't know the truth."

"What truth?"

Zak's lips pinched together, and he tugged on his ear, his expression conflicted. And then he sighed heavily. "Look, what I'm about to share with you, I probably should have told my sister first, but..." He shrugged. "Marin was cheating on Belle."

I jerked back in my chair as if I'd received an electric shock. "What did you say?"

Zak glanced at Chad, then returned his attention to me. "While I was in the hospital recovering from my injuries, a woman came to see me. She told me that she'd been seeing Marin for a few months and that he planned to break off his engagement to Belle but hadn't figured out how to tell her he'd fallen in love with someone else. He didn't want to hurt her, according to his lover." Zak snorted. "I told her to get out and that if she breathed a word to Belle, I'd spend the rest of my life making sure hers was ruined. She informed me that hurting Belle wasn't her intention at all, and she'd only told me in case, at some point in the future, I might think that Belle deserved to know. Now is that time."

I narrowed my eyes. "And you never told Belle any of this?"

"No."

"Jesus." I swept a hand down my face and blew out a steady breath.

"I think you should talk to her," Zak said. "Don't let Wyatt's nasty rhetoric get inside her head any more than it already has. She only told me today what happened on Monday, and only because I pressed her for answers. My sister is a thinker, and sometimes that's a good thing, but often, it's a bad thing. She disappears inside her mind and conjures up all sorts of shit that shouldn't be there."

I rubbed my fingertips over my lips, sparing Zak and Chad the odd glance while I pondered. "I'm sorry, Zak, but I can't. Belle deserves to keep her memories of her fiancé intact, and if that means she gives up on us..."

I shifted my gaze, unwilling to let Zak see the emotion in my eyes. "Then there's nothing I can do about that." I blinked to clear my vision, then refocused on him. "And you're not to tell her either."

"Okay," Zak said, but his tone didn't convince me.

"I mean it, Zak," I reiterated. "Those memories are precious, and she deserves to keep them."

Zak put his chair into reverse, signaling his intention to leave. "It was good to see you, Upton. Take care of yourself."

27

Belle

The trip to the animal shelter hadn't helped a bit. I thought walking a few dogs and cuddling a puppy or two might distract me for a couple of hours, but, if anything, it had made matters worse. When I'd poured out the whole sorry tale to Ariadne, she'd sided with both Upton and Zak and told me, in no uncertain terms, that the human heart was a complex beast, with no two the same, and therefore, no one should expect us to follow a cookie-cutter blueprint in our response to terrible grief.

She had a point, but one I wasn't quite ready to concede. Whenever I closed my eyes, Upton's hurt and puzzled expression on Monday night swam into view, and my stomach cramped up. I wanted to give us a chance, but I didn't know how to get back to him. It was as if I'd been taken out to sea in a boat, then tossed overboard and asked to swim back to shore. The harder I paddled, the farther away the shoreline got. I needed a catalyst, something that would propel me into action. Pride was an odd emotion. I loved Upton—yep, I'd finally, solidly, admitted that to myself—but I was scared to ask him to take me back in case he rejected me.

Stupid, right?

I trundled up our street, and as our house came into view, my gaze fell on Zak sitting on the front porch. As I approached, he motioned for me to join him.

"We need to talk," he stated.

I groaned. "Zak, please, stop nagging me. You're like a woodpecker drilling into a tree. You never stop."

He grinned. "True. And you also know that the fastest way to shut me up is to park your backside, open your ears, shut your mouth, and listen."

"I'm telling Mom," I whined, a homage to our past when, as kids, if I picked on Zak, he'd threaten to rat me out.

He laughed. "Good luck, she's out,"

I sat beside him and grasped the bottle of beer he passed to me from a cooler beside his chair. "It must be bad if you're plying me with drink."

Zak kept his lips pressed tight, and a twinge of anxiety pinched the soft lining of my gut. Something told me I wasn't going to like what he had to say. I took a long drink, then swung the bottle by its neck and touched mine to Zak's.

"Hit me with it, then."

"I went to see Wyatt."

"Zak!" I scolded. "You shouldn't have done that."

I wasn't all that surprised. Despite the challenges he faced with his disability, and the fact he was two minutes younger than me, he'd always gone to bat in my defense. My earliest memories were of Zak pushing one of our neighbor's kids to the ground because he pulled my pigtails as I was playing out in the street and made me cry. We were four at the time, and Zak had come barreling toward us, shoved both his palms into the boy's chest, and splat! Down he'd gone. His mother had come to see ours that night, outraged. Mom had told her to look a little closer to home for the problem, and maybe she should deal with her son's bullying behavior. Yeah, us Lakers stuck together.

Zak rubbed his forehead, and only then did I notice his grazed knuckles.

"What happened?"

He shrugged. "Not much. I took Chad with me."

At the mention of Zak's best friend, a powerhouse of a dude with a heart of gold, I flinched. "Please tell me Wyatt's still alive."

Zak threw back his head and laughed. "Yeah, he's alive. If I had to guess I'd say a broken nose from where I punched him, and a possible busted up jaw and a cracked rib or two that he has Chad to thank for."

I should feel bad that Wyatt had gotten hurt, but I didn't. Not in the slightest.

"Still sticking up for your big sis, huh, Zak?" I teased.

He snorted. "Two minutes older doesn't count."

"I disagree."

An ancient argument, but one that warmed me like an electric blanket on a cold winter's day. I leaned over and kissed Zak's cheek. He rubbed at the spot, then grinned.

"You shouldn't get any more trouble from Wyatt, but if you do, you'd better tell me."

I saluted. "Sir, yes, sir!"

He smiled faintly, then his face grew serious. "There's something else I need to tell you. I wasn't sure I'd ever need to have this conversation but I can't, in all good conscience, sit by and allow you to destroy what you have with Upton."

I sighed. "Zak, please."

He held up his hand. "Hear me out, and when you have, please try not to hate me."

A river of ice sped through my veins. There was nothing, *nothing,* that Zak could ever do that would make me hate him.

He was the other half of me, and no matter what he did, I'd love him until my last breath.

"Zak, you're scaring me."

His chest puffed out as he sucked in a lungful of air, and he reached for my hand. My heart raced, and sweat prickled across the nape of my neck, appearing out of fear rather than the warmth from the sun. I braced myself.

"Marin was cheating on you. Before he died."

It took a second or two for Zak's words to break through to my brain. The wooden porch beneath my feet swayed. *Are we having an earthquake?* Everything went silent, even the birds stopped tweeting. At least they did for me. Time skidded to a halt. Zak's lips were moving, but I couldn't hear him. My entire body trembled, my fingers jerking inside Zak's warm, solid hand.

"No," I rasped, pulling away from Zak. "You're lying."

His face crumpled. "I'd never lie to you."

Confusion propelled me to my feet. I turned my back and grabbed the hem of my shirt, scrunching it in my fist. It wasn't true. It *couldn't be true.* Marin had been one of the good guys, my childhood sweetheart, the only person outside of my close family unit I'd known with blinding clarity would never hurt me. I clamped a hand over my mouth, stuffing the impending cry deep inside of me.

"Belle?"

My throat tightened, and when I swallowed it hurt. My arms fell to my sides, limp and leaden, and my head felt too heavy for my neck. I let it drop. My eyes followed a trail of ants crawling across the porch, their purpose in life defined. Where was my purpose now? Everything I'd believed and trusted in was a lie.

"Belle."

Zak's tone sharpened, no doubt in a bid to get my attention. I held my hand up in the air.

"Give me a minute."

I stumbled into the house and headed straight for my bedroom. Just in time as it turned out because the second I got there, my knees went from under me and I sank onto the bed. Zak's revelation had opened a jagged wound in my chest, and I didn't know how to stitch it back together.

The whirr from Zak's wheelchair reached me, and seconds later, he appeared in the doorway, his expression wretched.

"I'm so sorry, Belle. I never wanted to hurt you, but I couldn't stand idly by and allow Wyatt to paint his brother as some kind of saint and you the wicked witch, and worse, have you believe those things to be true."

He came closer and extended his palm, allowing me the choice whether to take it or leave him hanging. I took the olive branch.

"How did you find out?"

He breathed in through his nose. "She came to see me at the hospital. The woman he'd been…" He trailed off. "Anyway, yeah, that's what happened."

I pinched the bridge of my nose, confused. "But why did she do that? What did she hope to gain?"

"She said that one day the time may come when you should know the truth, that he loved her and was planning to break off his engagement to you."

A surge of pain hit me squarely in the chest, so powerful, I doubled over, pressing a hand over my heart as if to hold it in. "It wasn't just a fling?" I whispered. "He wanted to end our relationship?"

Zak nodded.

"Oh God." I squeezed my eyes closed, hoping to hold in the tears. I failed.

"Belle."

Zak came as close as his chair allowed and pulled me into his arms. I collapsed against him, drawing on his strength. He remained silent while I cried, occasionally rubbing my back or stroking my hair.

Eventually, I straightened and gave Zak a wan smile. "I bet I look a terrible sight."

"Yeah, you do," Zak agreed.

I laughed. I actually laughed, despite the shock of learning that my first love, my fiancé, my childhood sweetheart, had cheated on me. See, this was what I loved about my brother. He always managed to bring a smile to my face, even in the worst of times.

"You're a jerk." Always a favorite of mine when it came to Zak.

"Get your insults in while I'm feeling generous," he said.

I laughed harder, and then I couldn't seem to stop. Zak joined in. We must have laughed for a good long minute, and I felt a whole lot better afterward.

"So, what about Upton?" Zak asked, as always straight to the point.

"I don't know, Zak." I shrugged. "What does this change, really?"

"Are you kidding me?" he exclaimed. "Belle, open your eyes, and I don't just mean to Marin's infidelity. You were fifteen when you got together with him. A child. I'm not denigrating what the two of you had together, but it wouldn't have lasted. Even if we hadn't gotten caught up in that bomb and Marin wasn't cheating on you, I'd have given it two years. If you dig deep and have an honest conversation with yourself, you will realize that what you feel for Upton is far more profound. It's the kind of love most people search their entire lives for. It's real, Belle."

"What Marin and I had was real," I insisted, but my voice wavered. Was it really? Or did Zak have a point that Marin and I drifted into a serious relationship, and Marin popping the question seemed like the logical next step?

"Not like you have with Upton," Zak reiterated. "Remember, sis, I've seen you with both these guys, and I know the difference between first love and true love. And come on, even you must agree that the fifteen-year-old you is vastly different from the twenty-three-year-old you. I know I'm hugely different, and I'm not talking about my disability. I'm talking about maturity."

I considered every word, carefully, slowly, taking my time to reflect and draw on my inner voice. To seek the truth in my heart. Zak's revelation regarding Marin's infidelity hurt. I couldn't deny that. But now that the shock had receded, I had to answer the question of whether I was more upset that I'd wasted so much remorse on a man who'd lied to my face and allowed me to ramble on about dresses and venues and bridesmaids while he figured out how he could extricate himself from a situation of his own making.

Even though I wanted to rush back into Upton's arms and tell him how sorry I was, and that I'd spend the rest of my life making it up to him, there remained, at the back of my mind, a niggle that he'd reject me. And he had every right to.

Still, there was only one true way to find out.

I rose from the bed and hugged Zak tightly.

"Thank you for telling me. That couldn't have been easy."

"It wasn't, but it had to be done. Now, please, tell me you'll speak to Upton."

I grinned. "Where do you think I'm going?"

Zak grabbed my wrist. "Before you do, there's one more thing. I went to see Upton today, after the altercation with Wyatt. You stubbornly refused to talk to him, and so I thought he might be the easier option to get you two back together. But he said no. Insisted you'd asked for space and he wanted to respect your wishes. And so I told him, about Marin. I'm sorry, sis. You deserved to be the first to know. I guess I hoped that if he knew, it might encourage him to make the first move.

Instead, he ordered me not to ruin your memories of Marin which I, of course, ignored."

Zak's admission should have angered me, but everything my brother did came from a place of love, and this was no different. I leaned down and kissed his cheek.

"Love you, bro."

28

Belle

My knees knocked together as I got off the bus and began the trek up the hillside to Upton's home. Several times I had to wipe my palms on my jacket—such class—and my heart bounced around in my chest as if it'd come unhooked from the arteries keeping it in place. I'd spent the bus ride over here practicing my speech, and even to me, it sounded lame. I could only hope Upton forgave me for unceremoniously dumping him on the cruel words of a man who'd never liked me anyway. I was more pissed off with myself than with Wyatt for allowing him inside my head and potentially ruining my chance at true happiness.

Zak told me that Upton was aware of Marin's affair. Zak's original plan had been for Upton to tell me, but he'd resisted. Smart man. If he'd told me, I'd have accused him of either making shit up to force my hand or ruining my memories, when the real culprit of the latter was Marin. I wasn't the kind of person to say he didn't deserve my sorrow—after all, I had loved him, and he'd loved me, once—but I'd spent enough time mourning him. It was time to move on, thanks to my annoying brother who'd opened my eyes to the truth.

The sight of Upton's imposing gates sent a fresh wave of dampness to my palms. At this rate, I'd have to toss my jacket in the trash. I stood there, my finger hovering over the buzzer, for at least thirty seconds. And then I remembered he had CCTV and the last thing I wanted was for him to see me standing here with my feet glued to the ground, unable to move. I could use the keypad to let myself in, but, in my opinion, that was overstepping the mark.

After taking three cleansing breaths, I rang the buzzer and waited. A few seconds later, Barbara's voice came over the intercom.

"Hello, Belle."

She sounded stiff and a bit cool. Not that I blamed her. Her loyalties lie with Upton, and no doubt she'd know we'd fallen out.

"Hey, Barbara. I'm here to see Upton. Is he in?"

"No, he's taken Bandit out for a walk, but he'll be back soon."

"Can I wait inside?"

A pause, then, "I suppose so."

The gates opened inward, and I walked through, unsure whether Upton's absence was a good or a bad thing. If he'd been inside, at least he'd have had the time it took me to arrive at the front door to prepare. Now, he'd end up blindsided. Still, there wasn't much I could do about that.

Barbara greeted me at the front door with a tight smile. She led me into the kitchen and, ever the perfect hostess, offered me a glass of iced tea which I refused. I was about to try to warm up the frosty atmosphere with an apology when the sound of the front door slamming drifted across the expansive hallway. My spine stiffened in anticipation, and I locked my gaze on the entrance to the kitchen. Bandit arrived first, his claws sliding on the tiled flooring. He bounded off the floor as if he had a trampoline beneath him and landed right in my arms, then proceeded to lick my face enthusiastically.

"Hey, little buddy." I scratched behind his ears. "I've missed you."

Upton's footsteps grew closer, and when he appeared, I could tell he hadn't been expecting me. He did a double take, his stare on the incredulous side.

"Belle. What are you doing here?"

I slid off the stool. "Can we talk?"

He nodded then cocked his head, indicating that I should follow him. I set Bandit on the floor, and he immediately dashed to his water bowl and started lapping furiously. I left him to it and followed Upton to the library. My gaze went to the door as he closed it behind me, and the slight smirk tugging at his lips said that's where his mind had gone, too.

"Memories, huh, Belle?"

I nodded as I perched on the edge of the couch. "Good memories."

"Are they?"

I rubbed my lips together and blinked up at him. He still hadn't taken a seat. "Zak told me. About Marin."

His expression hardened, and the amber of his eyes darkened to a burnished gold. "I expressly told him *not* to tell you."

"Yeah, well, that's Zak. He's always been a stubborn jerk."

I added a smile to show I was teasing, but Upton didn't bite. If anything, he appeared even angrier.

"So that's why you're here then? Because your brother told you your fiancé cheated on you. That's the only reason you've come here?"

I frowned. "I'm not sure I follow?"

"No?"

A trickle of unease began at the base of my spine, growing into a torrent that shot up to the nape of my neck.

"No. Look, what happened on Monday, I'm sorry, okay? Wyatt got inside my head and filled it with doubts, and I let him. That's on me. But—"

"But now that Zak's opened your eyes to the news of your fiancé's tarnished halo, you've decided that settling for second best might work after all."

My jaw fell open. I shook my head vigorously. "No, that's not it."

"Then what is it, Belle? Do enlighten me."

All my worries were morphing into reality in front of my very eyes, and if I didn't find a way to recover this situation, I'd lose the man I loved, and I'd have no one to blame but myself.

"I love you."

He snorted. *Snorted.* Not exactly the response I'd hoped for. But then a little voice whispered in my ear that when Upton had spoken those heartfelt words to me on Monday night, I'd followed up by leaving him. I deserved worse than a snort.

"It's true. I'd have come to that realization on my own eventually. All I asked for was a little time to work through the competing voices in my head, but I'd have gotten there without Zak's intervention. All he did was push me into acting earlier."

A speck of hope crossed his face, but then he schooled his expression, and goose bumps scattered down my arms at the sight of his cold stare. I rose to my feet and stood in front of him, preparing myself for rejection. If he backed away, I wasn't sure what I'd do.

He didn't. Instead, he breathed in through his nose and briefly closed his eyes, his body slightly angling toward mine.

"I've missed you," I whispered. "And I'm sorry. I'm so sorry for how badly I handled things. But I do love you. All I'm asking for is a chance to make it up to you, to prove that what I feel for you is so much deeper than what I had with Marin."

His startled expression gave me the courage to continue.

"Zak helped me see the truth. He showed me that the love I had for Marin was borne out of the innocence of a child who grew up alongside her best friend and just assumed he was the one. I think, deep down, I've known for a while that the feelings I have for you are very different to those I had for Marin. They're more intense, powerful. Passionate." I lowered my gaze. "But I didn't want to admit it, to you, or to myself. I couldn't shake the feelings of guilt, that somehow by acknowledging that you mean more to me than Marin ever did, that it compounded my betrayal. And so I buried my true feelings." I clutched his upper arms. "You have to believe that eventually, I'd have woken up to the truth. That I love you, mind, body, and soul. That the only people who can come between us are... us."

I fell silent, braced for rejection, despite my heartfelt admission.

Upton's forefinger knocked my chin up. "Look at me, Belle."

I slowly peered up at him through my lashes. His amber eyes flashed, but not from anger. I managed to take a quick breath, and then his mouth came down on mine, hard, demanding my full capitulation.

I happily ceded to this man, my one true love.

~

"Stop it!"

I scrambled away from Upton's relentless tickling, but he caught my ankle, dragging me back to bed, where he started up again with the tickles. Armpits, waist, hips, the soles of my feet. Nothing was off limits. Caught between hysterical giggles and wanting to punch him, I shoved at his barrel of a chest once more.

"I mean it. Either stop, or no more sex!"

The tickling came to a screeching halt, and he rocked back on his heels. "That'd better be a joke."

I laughed and pinched his nipple, hard enough to force a hiss between his teeth.

"Payback time."

I rolled off the bed and leaped to my feet, then danced around like a boxer trying to show their opponent they were dead meat. Upton burst out laughing at my antics.

It'd been like this between us for the past twenty-four hours, ever since we'd made up in the library. We were like a couple of teenagers who'd been given free rein of a house and were discovering each other for the very first time. The only time we'd left Upton's bedroom was to grab a bite to eat and check on Bandit. Even Barbara had beaten a hasty retreat, mumbling something about going to visit her sister who, Upton reliably informed me, lived in Chicago. A bit of a trek from LA.

"Shower, woman, now," Upton growled, pointing at the bathroom.

I skipped off, feeling lighter and happier than I had in years, maybe forever. I'd almost lost this man because of my own stupidity and stubbornness. If Zak hadn't taken a risk and told me about Marin, and despite what I'd said to Upton last night, maybe I would have spent the best years of my life full of remorse, unable to move forward.

My man came up behind me as I leaned into the stall and flicked on the shower. His erection pressed against my ass, and he circled his hips with a groan.

"I can't get enough," he murmured, his lips in my hair. "I might keep you locked in here forever."

"Sounds good." I pushed backward, eliciting another drawn-out groan.

He nudged me into the stall, and as the steam rose around us, he shifted me to face the wall. His large hands clasped my hips, and he lifted me and bent his knees. The head of his cock pressed to my entrance and he thrust inside, then instantly stilled.

"What's wrong?"

"Nothing." He swept my hair over my shoulder and kissed my neck. "I'm savoring you. The second I move, I'm gonna come."

"Lightweight." I clenched my inner muscles.

Upton hissed through his teeth. He trailed his hands up over my waist and cupped my breasts, pinching both nipples as hard as I'd done with his in retaliation for his tickling me. This time, it was my turn to hiss.

"Payback's a bitch, my sweet Belle," he said, and I felt his smile on my skin.

"Stop teasing me," I urged, wriggling against him.

"Ah, damn. You sure know how to get your own way."

With one hand on my hip, steadying me, he used his other to play with my clit and still managed to keep up an impressive rhythm, his hips bucking into me over and over. Despite what he'd said about coming, he waited for me to fall over the edge before allowing his own release.

The remnants of my climax still quivered between my legs as Upton pulled out of me then drew me around to face him. I curved my hands around his cheeks, noticing that he no longer flinched when I touched him there. To further test the theory, I traced his scar with the tip of my finger, then eased him around until his back was to me. Taking my time, I kissed every single scar while he braced his hands on the wall. I watched carefully for any signs of discomfort, but there were none.

When I finished tracing his scars with my tongue and my lips, he turned to face me, his amber eyes filled with awe.

"Thank you."

I tipped my head to the side. "What for?"

"For my life."

29

Belle

I waved Upton off to work, then jumped into my car, the one he'd gifted me on my first day at work. The same one I'd only driven for a day before giving it back after we briefly broke up. The last few weeks had exceeded all my hopes and dreams. Technically, I still lived at home with Mom and Zak, although as I'd slept here every night since making up with Upton, I guess it'd be fair to say I'd effectively moved in.

At the bottom of the hill, instead of turning left to go to work, today, I went right. Upton had no idea I'd taken the day off—thank goodness my new boss was understanding considering I'd not been there very long—but an idea had come to me a few days ago, and I'd been unable to shake it.

Upton deserved full closure for the event that changed his life, and mine, and ultimately brought us together. He told me the other night that I'd made his life complete, but there'd been a faint trace of regret in his eyes as he'd said it, and I had a very good idea why. Hence, I was headed the twenty miles inland to Westlake Village where Upton's father lived.

I parked on the street outside the Spanish-style red-roofed single-story home. The front yard was well tended with neatly mown grass and colorful borders, and a fountain at the center with a bird making use of the water by taking a bath.

After I cut the engine, I sat there for a few minutes to gather my thoughts, then climbed out. My heart was virtually in my throat as I knocked twice on the solid oak door.

The man who opened it looked so much like Upton, only an older version, I actually took a step back. In all the time I'd been with him, both as his companion and, later, as his lover, Upton's dad hadn't visited once, although Barbara told me he occasionally stopped by. Very occasionally, if ever, was my assessment.

"Mr. Barrick?"

He smiled kindly and nodded. "Yes, dear. What can I do for you?"

"Kyron, who is it?" A woman called out.

"Give me a second, Jenice."

He rolled his eyes, then winked. I hoped he was as genial when he realized who I was and why I'd come to see him.

"Mr. Barrick, my name is Izabelle Laker. I wonder if I might have a word. I'm your son's girlfriend, and I think it's time we talked."

His friendly smile fell, and he glanced over his shoulder. "I'm sorry, Miss Laker, but now isn't a good time."

"On the contrary, Mr. Barrick," I pressed. "It's the perfect time. You, and your wife, very much need to hear what I have to say."

He followed up another nervous glance behind him with a grimace. "Is he all right?"

I motioned with my chin, determined not to give him anything until he relented. "Why don't we go inside?"

Reluctantly, he stood back to allow me space to enter his home. He led me across a pristine tiled floor and into a large open-plan living space with vaulted ceilings, white-painted walls, and beautiful landscape pictures. Above the marble fireplace was a huge picture of Jenna that I recognized from the photographs in Upton's study. I glanced around, noticing the absence of any pictures of him.

A blonde woman dressed in a white jumpsuit with her hair immaculately styled gracefully rose to her feet. She shot a questioning look at her husband, then returned her attention to me.

"Jenice, this is Izabelle Laker," Kyron introduced. "Upton's girlfriend."

In my almost twenty-four years, I'd never seen someone's face change so quickly from one of open curiosity to obvious hostility.

"And you let her in because?" she spat at her husband.

"Mrs. Barrick, please. All I'm asking for is five minutes of your time."

"I don't want to hear it," she said, her bitter tone setting my teeth on edge as if I'd sucked on a lemon.

"Well, that's too bad, because you *are* going to hear me out," I said, my eyes daring her to challenge me.

She appeared a little taken aback, but my firm, determined tone sent her back to her seat. Upton's father gestured for me to sit.

"What can we do for you, Miss Laker?" he asked. "Did Upton send you here?"

I laughed. "Absolutely not. He wouldn't be at all happy with me if he knew I'd come to see you, but I happen to think what I have to say to you is worth risking his disapproval."

Jenice emitted a derisive snort. I chose to ignore it and focused on Upton's father instead. After all, he was the one I was here to convince, although I'd have to at least try to get Jenice on my side. She must have a lot of influence over Kyron considering he'd barely seen his only son—his only child now Jenna had gone—in the past year and a half.

He offered me a drink, which I declined, and after he'd taken a seat beside his wife, I began telling my story. They appeared surprised, clearly expected me to talk about Upton, but I had my reasons for beginning this way. They needed to understand that what happened wasn't Upton's fault, and the best way to get my point across, was to talk about Zak and Marin, and how my empathy for an elderly patient had such devastating effects on all our lives. But the biggest point I wanted to make was how Zak hadn't blamed me for his paralysis. Not once. He'd never railed on me or recriminated against me in any way.

Upton's father and stepmother listened in silence as I drew to a close.

"I understand the pain of losing your daughter, really I do, but blaming Upton when your anger should be directed at the terrorist who strapped a bomb to his chest and killed ninety-four people isn't fair. Upton is just as much of a victim as Jenna, as my brother Zak, as my fiancé, Marin. Just as much a victim as all those other innocent people whose lives were ended or changed forever by the cruel act of another."

I locked my gaze on his father and aimed my arrow.

"This is *your* son, Mr. Barrick. Your flesh and blood. I don't understand how you can cut him out of your life so easily. My brother wouldn't dream of treating me in such a way, and neither would my mother. She could have blamed me, too, yet all they did was shower me in love and affection." I shrugged one shoulder. "I guess they're just better people."

Jenice sucked in a sharp breath at my audacious remark, while Kyron's stricken and guilty expression should have made me feel bad.

It didn't.

It was about time someone told them both a few hard

truths, and I happily took on that mantle. It might not reconcile Upton with his father, but at least I'd know that I'd tried.

The silence lingered for a few moments, but as I made a move to stand, Kyron beat me to it.

"I want to see my son."

Jenice got to her feet, too. "Kyron—"

"No, Jenice," he said, cutting her off. "Whatever you're about to say, the answer is no." He lowered his chin, his eyes cast at the floor. "It's taken a stranger to open my eyes to the cruelty I've shown to my only son." He lifted his gaze to focus on his wife. "I'll never get over losing Jenna, and I know you won't either. I lost two children that terrible day, one at the hands of a terrorist, and one because I allowed you to persuade me that my son was somehow to blame. Well, no more."

Jenice blinked a few times, and then she began to cry. A quiet, resigned crying rather than excessive sobbing. "You're right, Kyron. I blamed Upton, and I convinced you to blame him, too. Directing my anger at Upton made the agony of losing my beautiful daughter a little easier to bear." She wrapped her arms around his waist and tucked her head underneath his chin. "It wasn't his fault. I know that. I'm just... I'm just so sad."

I'd closed off my emotions to come here and confront these people, but watching a mother's pain, still so raw, my heart opened up to her a little.

I took a few steps backward, unwilling to intrude on this private moment, but Kyron caught my movement and held up a single finger, indicating for me to stay. He comforted his wife for a few more minutes, then withdrew.

"I'd like to go and see my son now, Jenice."

She swept both hands beneath her eyes, drying her tears, and nodded. "Would you... tell him I said hello, and that I'm sorry. I hope that one day he can forgive me."

He gathered her into his arms and softly pecked her lips. "I will."

We agreed that Kyron would follow me to Upton's house in his car, and once we arrived, I'd call Upton and ask him to come home. During the entire journey, I wondered whether I'd made a huge mistake by interfering in Upton's family business. Upton rarely mentioned his father, and for all I knew, he was happy with the status quo. I didn't really believe that, but now that I'd put the wheels in motion, I'd started to doubt myself.

Too late now, Belle.

I settled Upton's father in the living room and made him a coffee, then called Upton. I reassured him nothing was wrong, but that I needed him to come home. I figured he mustn't have believed me when his car screeched to a halt at the front of the house forty minutes later when it should take him at least fifty-five to drive back home from the office.

"Christ, Belle, you're okay," he said, sweeping me into a hug.

"I told you everything was fine." I took hold of his hand and led him into the house. "You have a visitor."

He arched his eyebrows in surprise. "Oh, yeah? Who?"

I opened the door to the living room and gestured for him to go inside. The last thing I heard was his surprised exclamation of, "Dad?" before I closed the door to give them some privacy.

Two hours later, Upton found me hanging around in the library, reading a book. His face was drawn and tired-looking, and his hair stuck on end where he must have raked his fingers through it several times. He flopped onto the couch beside me and rested his head on my shoulder.

"He's gone."

I brushed a lock of hair off his forehead. "Are you mad at me?"

He lifted his head, meeting my worried gaze. "Not in the slightest. In fact, I want to thank you for pushing us together. We talked. He said some things. I said a lot more." He chuckled. "But I think we cleared a lot of the bad feelings."

"I'm glad."

His hand slid around the back of my neck, and he drew me down for a long, lingering kiss.

"He congratulated me on, and I quote, 'my feisty, forthright girlfriend'. Said you were a keeper."

"And what did you say?"

He grinned wickedly. "I said, I suppose she'll do."

30

UPTON

Belle turned onto her front, unclipped her bikini top, and handed me the bottle of sunscreen. "Would you rub some of this into my back?"

I set down the spy thriller that I'd tried to get into all week, but it hadn't really caught my attention. "If I must," I said, squeezing a dollop into my palm. "Although it's such a chore."

"Jackass," she muttered.

I massaged the cream into her soft skin, taking my time. Touching Belle was my favorite pastime. Well, apart from being inside her. That took the number one spot. With a quick glance around to check no one was watching, I slipped both hands underneath her and squeezed her tits. She giggled.

"That's not my back."

"No, it most certainly isn't. This, or I should say, these, are your gorgeous tits, and as soon as we return to our room for an afternoon nap, they will find themselves up close and personal with my mouth and my tongue."

"You're such a man."

I tugged at the waistband of my swim shorts and peered at my hard dick. "Yep. Definitely a man."

She laughed again. "Kiss me."

I pecked her lips, but as she deepened the kiss, I drew back. "You're playing a dangerous game. I'm hard, you're virtually naked, and Zak's nowhere in sight. We're practically alone."

"Except for the butler fetching our drinks."

"I'm sure he's seen worse." I reached for her hand and shoved it inside my shorts. "Go on then, as you insist. Just a quickie. It's your fault I'm always hard. You're too damn beautiful."

With a glance over her shoulder, she satisfied herself that we were, in fact, quite alone. And we had a good view. If anyone wandered over to check on us, we'd have enough time to make ourselves decent.

Her hand wrapped around my girth, and she pulled three times in quick succession. I groaned and joined her, covering her hand with mine. I dictated the pace, conscious we could be interrupted at any time, and I needed to come. Being around Belle gave me a constant itch I just had to scratch.

"Turn over," I murmured. "Let me see your tits."

"We can't."

"Yes, we can. I'm shielding you with my body. No one will see."

"It's against the law to sunbathe topless in Antigua."

"You're not sunbathing. You're having sexy times with your boyfriend. A boyfriend, I might add, who's rich enough to bribe the local police to turn a blind eye."

"If sunbathing topless is illegal, I'm absolutely sure that having sex in public isn't on the list of 'can do's'."

"We're not having sex."

She gave me one of her scolding looks but accompanied it with a headshake that had capitulation written all over it.

"If I end up in jail, you'd better come bail me out."

"Done."

She shifted onto her back. Her nipples were hard, begging for my tongue, and I bent my head and sucked one nub into my mouth, simultaneously encouraging her to rub me harder and grip me tighter.

"God, I'm close," I moaned.

"Fuck," she expelled.

"I know."

"No. Upton."

She removed her hand from my shorts and grabbed a towel, wrapping it around her body and stealing my view.

"Zak's coming."

"Lucky bastard."

She glared at me. "I mean he's on his way over. He's with that dolphin woman."

Despite my irritation at having an incredible orgasm ripped from me at the last moment, I chuckled. "You mean Shara."

The resort I'd chosen for a couple weeks' vacation catered specifically to disabled guests, involving them in all kinds of activities, one of which was swimming with dolphins, which Zak adored. All bets were off as to whether Zak's keenness to participate in that activity more than any other was solely down to the dolphins, or their trainer, a local Antiguan that Zak had taken a particular shine to.

Then again, if my hand were forced, I know where I'd put my money.

"I might have known you'd know her name," Belle groused.

I didn't have time to answer before we were no longer alone. Luckily my swim shorts were on the loose side. Just as well considering Belle's embarrassment had only served to make me even harder.

"Hey, Zak, Shara," I said. "Good swim?"

"Yeah."

Zak glanced up at his companion, and they shared a secretive look. I suppressed a grin. Swimming wasn't all they'd been up to.

"Um, listen, you guys," Zak began. His face reddened, and it wasn't because of the burning Caribbean sun. "I've asked Shara to have dinner with me tonight."

"Oh," Belle said. "I guess that's okay. Just let the butler know to set the table for four."

"Ah, yeah, no. I mean, we're going out for dinner. Just the two of us."

Belle's jaw dropped a good few inches. Her gaze lowered to where Shara's hands rested possessively on Zak's shoulders, and slowly it dawned on her.

Her brother had a date.

I chuckled and reached for her hand, drawing it to my mouth. "I'm sure your sister and I can keep ourselves busy in the meantime."

"Dude!" Zak exclaimed. "I'm begging you. Stop."

"I have to go, Zak," Shara said with a squeeze of his shoulder. "I have a couple of clients this afternoon. But I'll see you later. Eight, yeah?"

Zak's eyes softened as he looked up at her. "Can't wait."

"Me neither."

She hovered, almost as if she wanted to kiss him, but wasn't keen on the peanut gallery witnessing her private moment.

"Bye."

She waved, then ran off down the beach. Zak's eyes followed her until she disappeared from sight. Belle still hadn't found her voice, so I thought I'd help out a bit.

"Remember to take some condoms."

"I can't believe Zak's on a date," Belle said. "Ever since his accident, he's shown no interest in women."

"Maybe he was waiting for the right one to come along," I offered as I topped off her wine. "Like me."

She smiled lovingly. "That's a very valid point."

"Besides," I added, "you might be twins, but I'd lay odds on the fact he doesn't tell you everything. For all you know, he could have a ton of secret girlfriends."

"No, he doesn't," she said, looking more than a little annoyed that I dared to suggest such a thing.

I laughed. "You do realize that when he finally settles down, it'll be his wife that gets first dibs on his thoughts and feelings. You're going to have to learn to take a back seat."

"Don't." She groaned. "I can't bear it."

"He's had the same issue with us. Yet he's not nearly as put out as you seem to be. The glare you gave Shara when you realized they were going on a date." I swept a hand over my forehead. "Phew, the poor woman."

"Stop teasing me," she begged. "Goddammit, you're right. I hate the thought of my brother finding another confidant. Ugh. I'm a horrible sister."

"It's just as well he'll be living close by then," I said. "Where you can keep an eye on his comings and goings and vet any prospective future sister-in-law."

She wrinkled her nose. "What are you talking about?"

"I've bought a house down the street from ours. The workmen should have almost finished the alterations needed to ensure that it's suitable for Zak. When we get back, you can break the news."

"What?" She shook her head as if to eject water from her ears left over from our earlier swim. "Oh my God. You really bought them a house?"

"I told you when I asked you to move in that I'd make sure your family wasn't left behind. I'm aware how close you all are, and nothing makes me happier than when you're happy."

She jumped up from her chair, sat on my lap, wrapped her arms around my neck, and kissed me. "I love you so much."

"Enough to have sex on the beach?"

She laughed. "At the tenth time of asking, the answer remains no. I don't want to have to fish sand from a multitude of crevices for the next three weeks."

"Worth a try. The balcony, then. You owe me an orgasm from earlier when your brother interrupted us."

She got to her feet and extended her hand. "*That* I can agree to."

My phone rang before I took a step. I glanced at it. Sebastian. He could fuck off. A choice of talking to him or screwing my girlfriend? No contest.

But when it rang for the fourth time, Belle insisted I answer.

"If this isn't an emergency, I will kill you," I greeted him.

"How's the vacation?"

"Great. What do you want?"

"Okay, I get the hint. I'm calling about next week's board meeting."

"Fuck's sake, Seb. Can we worry about that next week?"

"Yeah, I need to give you a heads-up before Ryker calls you."

"About what?"

"Elliot."

I stiffened, sensing an undertone. "What about him?"

"He's off the rails, Upton. We lost the Saunders deal because he fucked up big time. Too busy chasing a ghost, and Ryker's patience has run out. At the next board meeting, he's going to motion to have Elliot removed from ROGUES, and he's made it clear that anyone who votes against him is effectively tendering their resignation. Technically he can't do that, but I think he said it to force us to take this seriously and back him. Elliot needs to wake up and smell the goddamn coffee before he takes us and the company we've worked our asses off to build down with him."

My heart plunged to the weathered wood beneath my feet, fear for Elliot, for ROGUES, for our years-long friendship stealing the air from my lungs.

"Oh fuck."

THE END

Fifty Million Dollars.

That's how much my sister's freedom cost.
She's moved on. I haven't.
I think about the horror of her kidnapping every day. Every hour. Every goddamn second.

Someone has to pay.

Yet despite my relentless searching, each road leads to a dead end.

Until a chance meeting with my secret high school crush changes everything.

She promises answers where I only have questions.
She vows to support me on my quest for justice.

Except I'm on a path to self-destruction, and if she's not careful, I'll take her down with me.

***

A lot can happen in a decade and a half.

I'm no longer the shy, awkward girl who blended into the background. And he's no longer the guy who excelled at everything.

He's bitter and angry and filled with a thirst for revenge.

Yet despite the intervening years, those suppressed feelings of lust reappear.

But he's dangerous, and if I allow myself to become embroiled in his desire for payback, I might just lose myself.

Tennis heartthrob Cash Gallagher is undefeated both on and off the court. But beneath his superstar playboy image, he's hiding a painful secret. When a headline-busting exposé hits a little too close to home, he's determined to match the feisty journalist swing for swing.

Tally McKenzie is one story away from launching her career into the big leagues. But when her unauthorized tell-all triggers his infamous competitive streak, she'll go toe to toe with the man of her dreams for a shot at fame and a fantasy of her own.

As their flirtatious rivalry heats up, can Cash and Tally drop their defenses and let love in or will old doubts and dark secrets ruin their perfect match?

ACKNOWLEDGMENTS

I owe so much to my wonderful team who cheer me on, encourage me every step of the way, and challenge me to dig deep to make every novel I release the very best it can be.

I love you all - and in no particular order...

To hubs - thank you for supporting me in following my dreams. I know it's not always easy, especially when my mind wanders when you're trying to talk to me. Your patience with how much my characters overtake me at times knows no bounds. Love you to bits.

To my critique partner, Incy... Thank you so much for your critique. You really force me to take a second look at things and while we don't agree on everything, you know and I know that I'll have thought long and hard about your advice. I'd hate to do this without you.

To my amazing, funny, kind, generous, wonderful PA, Loulou. Thank you for always being in my corner.

Emmy - thank you for your brilliant editing as always. I appreciate the heck out of you and am so glad you're my editor.

Katie - gah! I love you and appreciate you so much. Sorry about the cliffy (again)! Zak says thank you for the job!

Jean - I love you. Love love love. Sorry about the habit I'm forming (LOL). But it's just so much fun! Remember to send me the picture of your Eton Mess.

Jacqueline - Thank you for reading, as always. The things you still pick up despite all the eyes on my manuscript is astounding. You're awesome.

To my ARC readers. You guys are amazing! You're my final eyes and ears before my baby is released into the world and I appreciate each and every one of you for giving up your time to read.

And last but most certainly not least, to you, the readers. Thank you for being on this journey with me. It still humbles me to think that my words are being read all over the world.

If you have any time to spare, I'd be ever so grateful if you'd leave a short review on Amazon or Goodreads. Reviews not only help readers discover new books, but they also help authors reach new readers. You'd be doing a massive favor for this wonderful bookish community we're all a part of.

ABOUT TRACIE DELANEY

Tracie Delaney realized she was destined to write when, at aged five, she crafted little notes to her parents, each one finished with "The End."

Tracie loves to write steamy contemporary romance books that center around hot men, strong women, and then watch with glee as they battle through real life problems. Of course, there's always a perfect Happy Ever After ending (eventually).

When she isn't writing or sitting around with her head stuck in a book, she can often be found watching The Walking Dead, Game of Thrones or any tennis match involving Roger Federer. Coffee is a regular savior.

You can find Tracie on Facebook, Twitter and Instagram, or, for the latest news, exclusive excerpts and competitions, why not join her reader group.

Tracie currently resides in the North West of England with her amazingly supportive husband and her two crazy Westie puppies, Cooper and Murphy.

Tracie loves to hear from readers. She can be contacted through her website

www.authortraciedelaney.com

Printed in Great Britain
by Amazon

74483441R00147